Staring at the Future

The Chronicles of Kerrigan: Gabriel, Volume 3

W.J. May

Published by Dark Shadow Publishing, 2017.

This is a work of fiction. Similarities to real people, places, or events are entirely coincidental.

STARING AT THE FUTURE

First edition. November 12, 2017.

Copyright © 2017 W.J. May.

Written by W.J. May.

Also by W.J. May

Bit-Lit Series
Lost Vampire
Cost of Blood
Price of Death

Blood Red Series
Courage Runs Red
The Night Watch
Marked by Courage
Forever Night

Daughters of Darkness: Victoria's Journey
Victoria
Huntress
Coveted (A Vampire & Paranormal Romance)
Twisted

Hidden Secrets Saga
Seventh Mark - Part 1
Seventh Mark - Part 2
Marked By Destiny

Compelled
Fate's Intervention
Chosen Three
The Hidden Secrets Saga: The Complete Series

Paranormal Huntress Series
Never Look Back
Coven Master
Alpha's Permission

Prophecy Series
Only the Beginning
White Winter
Secrets of Destiny

The Chronicles of Kerrigan
Rae of Hope
Dark Nebula
House of Cards
Royal Tea
Under Fire
End in Sight
Hidden Darkness
Twisted Together
Mark of Fate
Strength & Power
Last One Standing
Rae of Light
The Chronicles of Kerrigan Box Set Books # 1 - 6

The Chronicles of Kerrigan: Gabriel
Living in the Past
Staring at the Future
Present For Today

The Chronicles of Kerrigan Prequel
Christmas Before the Magic
Question the Darkness
Into the Darkness
Fight the Darkness
Alone in the Darkness
Lost in Darkness
The Chronicles of Kerrigan Prequel Series Books #1-3

The Chronicles of Kerrigan Sequel
A Matter of Time
Time Piece
Second Chance
Glitch in Time
Our Time
Precious Time

The Hidden Secrets Saga
Seventh Mark (part 1 & 2)

The Senseless Series
Radium Halos

Radium Halos - Part 2
Nonsense

Standalone
Shadow of Doubt (Part 1 & 2)
Five Shades of Fantasy
Shadow of Doubt - Part 1
Shadow of Doubt - Part 2
Four and a Half Shades of Fantasy
Dream Fighter
What Creeps in the Night
Forest of the Forbidden
HuNted
Arcane Forest: A Fantasy Anthology
Ancient Blood of the Vampire and Werewolf

The Chronicles of Kerrigan: Gabriel
Staring at the Future
Book 3
By W.J. May
Copyright 2017 by W.J. May

THIS E-BOOK IS LICENSED for your personal enjoyment only. This e-book may not be re-sold or given away to other people. If you would like to share this book with another person, please purchase an additional copy for each recipient. If you're reading this book and did not purchase it, or it was not purchased for your use only, then please return to Smashwords.com and purchase your own copy. Thank you for respecting the hard work of the author.

All rights reserved. No part of this publication may be reproduced, stored in or introduced into a retrieval system, or transmitted, in any form, or by any means (electronic, mechanical, photocopying, recording, or otherwise) without the prior written permission of both the copyright owner and the above publisher of this book.

This is a work of fiction. Names, characters, places, brands, media, and incidents are either the product of the author's imagination or are used fictitiously. Any resemblance to actual person, living or dead, events, or locales is entirely coincidental. The author acknowledges the trademarked status and trademark owners of various products referenced in this work of fiction, which have been used without permission. The publication/use of these trademarks is not authorized, associated with, or sponsored by the trademark owners.

All rights reserved.
Copyright 2017 by W.J. May
Cover design by: Book Cover by Design

No part of this book may be used or reproduced in any manner whatsoever without written permission, except in the case of brief quotations embodied in articles and reviews.

Have You Read the C.o.K Series?

The Prequel series is a Sub-Series of the Chronicles of Kerrigan.
The prequel on how Simon Kerrigan met Beth!!
Download for FREE:

The Chronicles of Kerrigan: PREQUEL –

CHRISTMAS BEFORE THE Magic
    Question the Darkness
    Into the Darkness
    Fight the Darkness
    Alone in the Darkness
    Lost the Darkness

The Chronicles of Kerrigan

BOOK I - *Rae of Hope* is FREE!
　Book Trailer:
　http://www.youtube.com/watch?v=gILAwXxx8MU
　Book II - *Dark Nebula*
　Book Trailer:
　http://www.youtube.com/watch?v=Ca24STi_bFM
　Book III - *House of Cards*
　Book IV - *Royal Tea*
　Book V - *Under Fire*
　Book VI - *End in Sight*
　Book VII – *Hidden Darkness*
　Book VIII – *Twisted Together*
　Book IX – *Mark of Fate*
　Book X – *Strength & Power*
　Book XI – *Last One Standing*
　Book XII – *Rae of Light*

The Chronicles of Kerrigan SEQUEL

MATTER OF TIME
    Time Piece
    Second Chance
    Glitch in Time
    Our Time
    Precious Time

The Chronicles of Kerrigan: Gabriel

Living in the Past

Present for Today

Staring at the Future

Find W.J. May

Website:
http://www.wanitamay.yolasite.com
Facebook:
https://www.facebook.com/pages/Author-WJ-May-FAN-PAGE/141170442608149
Newsletter:
SIGN UP FOR W.J. May's Newsletter to find out about new releases, updates, cover reveals and even freebies!
http://eepurl.com/97aYf

Staring at the Future Blurb:

HAPPY ENDINGS ARE JUST stories that haven't been finished yet.

When the girl he loves is kidnapped by the same man who killed his father Gabriel's newfound bliss vanishes in a heartbeat, and he finds himself slipping into old habits. The love-struck romantic is put on a shelf so the stone-cold assassin can come out to play.

Reinforcements are called, and old friends make sudden new appearances as an old enemy finally reveals himself.

Have the shadows chasing Gabriel finally caught up with him? Is the darkness in his past strong enough to overtake his future? Has he changed enough to get his own happily ever after? Or is it just another bad memory?

The players are ready, the board is set. All that's left to do is play the game...

Chapter 1

THE PREVIOUS YEAR, over fourteen thousand people were reported missing in New York City. Well over half of those were women. Well over half of those were under the age of twenty-five. In the grand scheme of things, the world wasn't changed much by the sudden disappearance of one girl.

But Gabriel's world? Gabriel's world came to a screeching halt.

The second he walked in the door, he walked right back out again—striding into the grimy hallway in a burst of speed. His eyes tightened with an emotion that threatened to overwhelm as he wrapped his arm over his mouth to stifle a ferocious scream. There was a quiet creaking across the hall as the woman who lived next door opened her door a crack to peer outside. One look at his face and she slammed it shut again, bolting the lock for good measure.

He didn't even register her presence.

A sharp kick to the wall then he sank down against it, burying his face in his hands as he tried to get a hold of himself. His heart was pounding in quick, uneven bursts, and no matter how many times he tried he was unable to catch his breath. All his usual tricks and techniques failed him, replaced with a chilling mantra. One that echoed louder and louder in his head.

They took her. HE took her. He has her RIGHT NOW.

The walls themselves started to tremble. The metal pipes beneath them groaned and threatened to burst. On the other end of the hallway the elevator shook precariously against its supports, the metal doors caving in as the box dangled over a ten-story drop.

"What's happening?!"

"Are we having an earthquake?!"

Voices started calling out from apartment to apartment. Rising with panic as the very foundations of the building trembled and shook. Fortunately, none of them had the sense to look outside and see that the rest of the world was steady. Instead they whipped out their phones, updated their social media status to 'feeling doomed,' and then probably huddled in their bathroom doorways.

The only person to remain unaffected was the man crouching against the hallway wall. His hands clenched into manic fists and his green eyes burning a hole in the floor.

Get a grip, Gabriel! You've got to get back in there! You've got to think!

For the first time in his life, Gabriel was unable to do so. For the first time in his life the logic and reason centers of his brain shut down completely, leaving nothing but a tangle of raw emotions underneath. He had become one of those people he'd always hated. The kind that stood gawking on the wrong side of the police tape. A helpless bystander, uselessly sidelined.

That inner voice tried again. Appealing to the side of him that had recently vowed to try to avoid mass murder. *Calm down and breathe, or all these people are going to die.*

It was a valiant effort, but it fell on deaf ears. At the moment Gabriel couldn't care less if everyone in the building, the borough, or even the entire city fell prey to a fiery demise. His only concern was with one particular life. A life that was holding his undivided attention. Distracting him to the point of frenzy as the walls around him splintered and cracked.

Then that voice said the only thing in the world that could possibly make a difference.

You're wasting time.

All at once, the quaking stopped. The foundations of the building settled, and the world was suddenly very still. Gabriel pushed to his feet. A little dizzy, a little shaken, but seized with a wide-eyed determination as he moved back inside.

It was impossible to be objective, but he sincerely tried. Impossible to approach the situation dispassionately, he gave it everything he had—compartmentalizing as best he could while he made a slow rotation around the apartment.

Every piece of shattered glass was a clue. Every overturned table told a story.

His sharp eyes missed not a single detail as he turned in a slow orbit, cataloguing everything he saw to memory. Then he went back and did it all over again.

She'd put up a struggle, that much was clear. In fact, by the looks of things she'd put up a hell of a fight. The mirror in the bathroom was still clouded with the faintest hint of steam from her morning shower but her dresser drawers were askew, so she'd had time to get dressed again before colliding with her attacker. The coffee maker was full of water but the brew itself had yet to be poured, meaning she was most likely in the kitchen when the man kicked down the door. A door which still hung in broken pieces on the splintered frame.

Gabriel's muscles coiled with rage as he followed the grisly trail from one room to the next, reading the chaos with the skill of one who'd had to do it too many times before.

The main fight had happened in the living room, after the man grabbed her and was dragging her back to the front door. There was a clear trail of wreckage, dotted with smears of blood from where she'd tried to get away by grabbing onto everything in sight. A broken fingernail was wedged in the bookshelf. A lock of hair was caught in the frame by the door.

Finally, Gabriel came to the last piece of the puzzle. A crumpled handkerchief, half-kicked beneath the overturned coat rack. With depressingly practiced hands, he knelt to the floor and gingerly picked it up. Giving it a detached sniff, he quickly dropped it back to the floor.

Chloroform.

The sweet, sickly smell barely masked the harsh stench of chemicals just underneath. It was an inelegant tool, but highly effective. Given the amount of fight she'd apparently put up, it was likely the only thing in the world guaranteed to stop her incessant screaming.

The fabric had been doused. Either they were intending for her to sleep a long time, suggesting a safe-house outside the perimeter of the city, or the man pouring it simply had a heavy hand. Gabriel didn't know the skill level of the people he was dealing with. The man he'd encountered in the subway hadn't put up much of a fight, and the people he'd seen in the market had clearly been drawn to Stryder based on nothing but blind loyalty and intimidation.

In a way, that made things even worse.

Gabriel was used to dealing with people whose skill and talent matched his own. People who didn't make mistakes, or leave trails of breadcrumbs to follow. People who would have had the good sense to set the handkerchief on fire, rather than leaving it on the floor.

STARING AT THE FUTURE

Those people, he understood. *Those* people, he'd spent a lifetime tracking. It was the entire reason Cromfield had trained him all those years. To beat the unbeatable. To take the impossible missions. To solve the cases that no one else could.

The fact that he could be dealing with amateurs made the entire situation that much less predictable. Opened each clue to a hundred new questions and interpretations. Ones that didn't come as easily. Ones that took entirely too much time.

Time I don't have...

Gabriel stared around the apartment for a second more before crouching to think. The band of thugs might be a wild card, but he knew Stryder. He wouldn't go back to the apartment where Gabriel had first found him—that place would be long-deserted. And he wouldn't risk leaving the city. Car rentals and flights left a paper trail that would be too easy to track. Then there was the fact that Stryder had chosen New York. He'd actually worked to build a life there, just as surely as Gabriel had worked to build one in London. He didn't want to leave the city. He didn't want to burn whatever bridges he'd made. He simply wanted to bide his time, lying low, and trusting that—whenever Gabriel found him—he'd be ready.

Which brought Gabriel back to square one.

Almost nine million people in the city. Five boroughs. Three hundred and five square miles. A subterranean labyrinth with an endless array of places to hide.

Back when he was working with Cromfield, he had an entire underground network. An intricate system of people embedded throughout the whole of western Europe, who he would activate in times like this. People who kept their ears to the ground. People who knew the stories before they went to print. People who could be counted on to shut down the entire London Planetarium just to pilfer a docent's uniform by Cromfield's unreasonable five a.m. deadline.

Granted, that last one had only happened the one time...

But Gabriel didn't know this city. He didn't know this country. The majority of people with ink had stayed somewhere on the European continent, and it wasn't often that his work had brought him to America's shores. Even if he could resurrect one or two of his old contacts, they were unlikely to help him now. Not after he was rather famously working for the other side.

"Where are you?"

He said the words aloud, muttering them feverishly to himself as he cupped his hands over his lips, deep in thought. Again and again, ideas failed him. Over and over, his plots and schemes fell short and he was left searching once again for a place to start.

What I need is a tracker. I don't have any pictures of Natasha to send to Kraigan, and for all I know Jules is still trapped in Iceland while Devon works out a travel visa. Even if I was somehow to get in contact with Rae, there just isn't time—

It hit him like a ton of bricks. Here he was, stuck in New York, without the use of a tracker. But hadn't Peter said that *he* was a tracker? It was a bit hard to remember through the blood loss and disorientation of those first few days, but he was almost sure.

A tiny flicker of hope stirred deep in his eyes. Yes, Peter was a tracker. That's how he and Canary had found him bleeding out in Stryder's building.

That's how I'm going to get Natasha back.

The second he thought her name he was back on his feet, flying through what was left of her crumbling apartment as he raced into the hall. He didn't stop running until he was back on the sunny New York City sidewalk. The wind in his hair, and the bright morning light beating down upon his face.

It seemed like only a few moments ago that he was leaving the apartment for the first time. Waking up in the bed of a beautiful woman. Strolling down the city streets to buy her flowers, as happy as he'd ever been. How was this possibly still the same morning?

It was a testament to what a blind panic Gabriel was in, that he didn't think twice about taking the subway. He simply leapt over the ticket counter and darted into the crowd, pushing people rudely out of his way just in time to leap aboard the departing train. From there, it was a terrible waiting game. Drumming his fingers impatiently against the metal pole as the train stopped again and again to let passengers on and off. Living and dying with each stop.

By the time he finally arrived at his own platform, there was a wide berth around him. New Yorkers had a keen sense for crazy, and in that moment Gabriel was running with the very best of them. They watched with casual interest as he manically shoved his way towards the door. As his hand twitched and it seemed to open a little earlier than usual. As he leapt onto the open platform and darted away up the stairs, his golden hair soon lost in the crowd.

He was greeted with the familiar sound of city sirens as he raced into the sunlight once more, taking a second to get his bearings before sprinting away up the street. Trying to calm himself with the knowledge that the Chinese restaurant where he and Fischers lived was only a few blocks away. He'd be there in a matter of minutes. In a matter of *minutes*, he'd know where Natasha was and would then proceed to move Heaven and Hell to get her back.

Even in his present state of mind, he couldn't help but realize how intensely lucky he was. Trackers like Peter were few and far between. Brooklyn couldn't have many. Not only had the man already saved Gabriel's own life with his gift, but now he was going to help him find...

Gabriel's hair flew out in front of him as he came to a sudden stop, freezing dead still in the middle of the road. No, Brooklyn couldn't have many trackers. Peter was a rare target indeed.

It was at that moment he suddenly realized where those sirens were headed...

BY THE TIME GABRIEL got to the restaurant, the place was in ruins. Smoke was spiraling from the dilapidated roof, and streams of water were still running down the bricks from where the fire department had attempted to put out the devastating flames.

All the fight and fire drained right out of him as he froze on the spot. It was replaced with a dull sort of numbness, one that started in his feet and worked its way slowly up the rest of his body.

"Excuse me." He could hardly recognize his own voice as he caught a woman standing next to him by the elbow. "Do you know what happened here?"

"It was an electrical fire," she responded promptly, holding up her phone to take a picture of the ash-covered rubble. "Lit the whole place up before anyone could stop it. Real shame."

Gabriel blinked slowly at the burnt-out building, palsied with shock. "...what?"

The woman turned, flashing him a tight smile. "I said it's a real shame. I used to get noodles from this place. It was really good."

He shot her a look of disbelief before tentatively weaving his way through the crowd. A police barrier was already in place, and the scene was swarming with officers. Stomping in and out of the scorched doorway, their heavy boots left thick stains on Magda's tiled floor.

A tiny surge of anger fought its way through that deadening numbness as he made his way to the very front, slipping noiselessly under the caution tape at the same time.

"Excuse me!" A heavy hand clamped down on his shoulder. "Just where do you think you're going? That was a *police barricade* you just ignored."

Gabriel shook through his trance to find himself staring into the eyes of one of New York's finest. A man who obviously relished the opportunity to flash that badge and unroll that damn yellow tape whenever possible.

It shouldn't have been a problem. Gabriel had bypassed the police many times before. At this point, they were hardly more than a logistical nuisance. A minor stepping stone on the way to getting whatever it was he wanted at the time.

Your training. Remember your training. You've got a lifetime of it.

Speak with confidence. Distract with vague questions. Claim to have come at the request of some authority figure above his head. By the time he looks back, you're already gone.

Cromfield 101.

It shouldn't have been a problem, yet somehow it was. For the first time, those duplicitous instincts failed him, and for the life of him Gabriel couldn't think of a single word to say. When he finally did manage to speak, he was clumsy. Quiet. Unconvincing.

"I...I used to come here." He stared helplessly into the burned-out interior of the dining room. The fire was gone, but he could still feel the heat. "I know these people."

The man softened a bit, and his grip on Gabriel's shoulder loosened. His tone, however, was as unyielding as ever. "This is a crime scene, son. It's best you go on your way."

Gabriel stared over his shoulder for a second more before the officer gave him a pointed shove in the other direction. His breath caught in his chest and he nodded quickly, that same paralyzing numbness holding him firmly in its grasp.

"...okay."

He took a few steps back, his hands trembling as they lifted the tape once again, when a sudden voice called out to him from somewhere inside the restaurant.

"...Gabriel?"

In a flash, he was all momentum. Ignoring the officer completely. Pushing past the confused firemen. Forcing his way inside. For a second, he couldn't make out where the voice was coming from. Then he saw her.

Magda was lying on the ground behind a pile of broken tables. An EMT had been kneeling there with her, but judging by the look on the man's face, and the fact that they weren't trying to move her, there was nothing more they could do.

Peter was already dead. Slumped over the countertop just a few yards away. An oddly peaceful look on his face as he reached towards his wife.

It was one of those moments Gabriel knew he would remember forever. The kind that burned itself into his memory, even as he saw it for the first time. A rush of horror washed over him, but his legs moved forward robotically—not stopping until he was kneeling on the floor beside her, holding her bloody hand.

"Gabriel..." she said again, fainter than the first time. Her face cracked into a weak smile as she gripped his fingers as tightly as she could. "You're alive. Peter and I were so worried."

"*You* were worried about *me*?" Gabriel's heart broke a thousand times over, and a small part of him wondered if he'd ever be able to stop hating himself. "*I* did this, Magda. If I hadn't come here, none of this would have happened—"

"You can't think about it that way." She shook her head painfully, coughing up a mouthful of blood. "These were bad men. You came here to do something good."

Gabriel shook his head, squeezing her hand tighter as a sudden tear slipped down his face. "I'm so sorry. I can't even tell you how sorry—"

"*Shh*." She pressed a finger over his lips, her eyes glassing over with that same smile as she lay her head back down on the floor. "Remember, honey, some people get saved. Some people do the saving. You, Gabriel Alden, are the latter."

"Magda," he whispered. "Magda, please don't—"

But it was too late. She was already dead.

It happened so quickly that no one else noticed. Gabriel's mouth fell open, but he was unable to make a sound. Unable to let anyone know. Unable to let go of her hand. It was like someone had placed their hands over his ears, giving the smoky room a strange, dreamlike quality. Muffling the abrasive sounds. It wasn't until the EMT turned back around and yelled something indecipherable that Gabriel let go, suddenly pushing back to his feet.

This time he didn't need the police to evict him; he couldn't get away fast enough. He was under the barricade and around the corner before anyone inside was the wiser, moving quickly down a narrow alley, away from the gawking crowd. The second he could no longer hear the noise he slid down against the side of the building, his body freezing up in shock.

It wasn't that he was a stranger to death. He'd watched enough people die to last him several lifetimes. It wasn't the blood, or the sirens, or the fake-fire, or the fact that all those bustling policemen had already deemed what was double-homicide nothing more than an electrical accident.

It was the people he had lost. The beloved couple lying dead inside.

...because of me.

He was responsible for this. All of this. Every drop of blood, every gasping breath. He knew what kind of person he was, he knew the kind of danger that followed him, yet he had brought it into their lives. Like a child swimming too close to a current, he had sucked them down with him. Yet another casualty in his tale of tragedy and loss. Another chapter in the story.

As if to haunt him, he heard an echo of Magda's last words. That he was some sort of savior. That the men who did this were bad people, but he had come there to do good.

Except I didn't. I came to New York to kill a man. A man who is systematically destroying all the people I've come to love.

And speaking of...

The phone was in his hand before he even thought to dial the number. It was ringing just a second after that. For a terrified moment, he held his breath. Then a crackling, Southern-accented voice came on the other line.

"Hello? Gabriel Alden, are you stalking me?"

He let out a sigh of relief, paired with a belated sob. "Eliza, are you all right? Where are you?"

There was a brief pause, and her voice tightened with concern. "Well, I'm visiting my sister for a few days upstate. I told you I was leaving at dinner, don't you remember?"

No, he most certainly didn't remember. The travel plans of the old and restless were of very little concern to him, but he was admittedly thrilled to hear them now.

"No, I...I must've forgotten." He ran his free hand back through his hair, trying to get a grip on himself. "Well, that's great. You have a good time there, all right?"

"Gabriel, what's going on?" There was not an ounce of humor in her voice. Not a hint of that perpetual mischief he'd come to expect. "Something's wrong, I can hear it in your voice."

"Nothing's wrong," he said quickly. "I just...I've been reading that journal again. I think you were right, I should just stop."

It was a believable excuse, said in a passable tone. After a moment's consideration, Canary seemed to accept it. "Honey, I'm so glad to hear it. Just put that book away. All it does is bring you trouble. Go out and enjoy the summer sunshine. Maybe bring Natasha..."

Another tear slipped down his face and he nodded, clenching the phone in his hand. "Yeah...yeah, I think I will. Have fun with your sister. Take your time."

"Stay out of trouble, now."

The line clicked off, but it was quite a while before Gabriel lowered the phone away from his ear. It was quite a while before he slipped it back into his pocket, and it was even longer still before he pushed to his feet, starting the slow walk back to Natasha's apartment.

IT WAS FOUR IN THE morning. Four in the morning, but Gabriel had yet to fall asleep. Truth be told, he had yet to even close his eyes. Not that he was trying. For the last nine hours, he had been sitting fully clothed in Natasha's bathtub.

His eyes stared unblinkingly at the door as his mind raced a million miles a minute, thinking of everything and nothing at the same time. He could still smell faint traces of vanilla and lavender from the bath they'd shared together the night before. If he listened hard enough, he could still hear her magical laugh echoing happily off the cold tiles.

How could they have taken her? How could *he* have let it happen? Was he really so caught up in his own happiness that he failed to sense the danger approaching? Had he really let down so many walls and defenses that he'd failed to protect the people he loved?

They won't kill her. Not yet.

It was his only solace. The last remaining hope, giving him some small semblance of sanity. He knew Stryder well enough by now to be certain. Natasha was a bargaining chip. It would serve no purpose if she was dead.

Not that it was much of a comfort. There were plenty of things out there worse than death. Gabriel knew that better than most. If he wanted to save Natasha from that same, cold darkness—the next move would be his.

A sudden noise outside roused his attention. The soft crunch of light footsteps. Two pairs of boots, carefully making their way down the hall.

Gabriel didn't stop to think. Didn't make an active decision to move. The second he heard the sound he was on his feet, ghosting across the apartment like a dark spirit. Propelled by nothing but sheer adrenaline as he hovered breathlessly behind the front door.

It was unlocked. He'd left it that way. Daring the people who'd broken it in the first place to come back inside. He could think of nothing he wanted more in the entire world.

There was a quiet pause before the handle turned. Another pause and it pushed open slowly—letting in a thin stream of light from the hall.

For a second, all was quiet. Then the room was a blur of motion.

Twenty years of training kicked in as Gabriel leapt high in the air, catching the first man who walked through the door with a sharp kick across the face. There was a soft cry as he crumpled to the floor. The other was still gasping in surprise, when Gabriel caught him by the collar and yanked him through the door, pinning him roughly against the wall.

"Where is she?!" he shouted, just a breath away from killing the man right where he stood. "Tell me where she is, or I swear I'll..."

He trailed off in shock, staring into the dark with wide eyes.
"...Devon?"

Chapter 2

DEVON WARDELL WAS FROZEN dead still, staring back in shock with his arms hanging limp at his sides. On the other side of the room Julian was slowly getting to his feet, rubbing tenderly at his jaw where Gabriel had kicked him.

"I don't understand." Gabriel didn't relax his position for a moment; he was just as stunned as the rest of them. "How are you—"

"Jules had a vision," Devon breathed, still completely unable to move. A halo of cracked plaster spider-webbed out from where his head had made a small crater in the wall, and the moonlight pouring in from the window painted his tan skin a ghostly shade of white.

It took Gabriel a second to realize the problem wasn't that Devon wasn't able to move, but that Gabriel wasn't letting him. He took a step back at once, releasing his friend's collar and giving his shirt a cursory straightening. "I'm sorry," he mumbled, swiftly backing away. "I didn't…I thought you were…"

He didn't stop moving until the backs of his shoes touched the far wall. Too much had happened in the last twenty-four hours, too much had gone wrong. And for one of the first times in his life, he was having trouble keeping up.

Devon peeled himself off the wall, looking his friend up and down with the sort of caution one would use when approaching a wild animal. "Gabriel…what happened?"

It was clear something had gone wrong. If the ravaged apartment wasn't enough, one look at Gabriel's face would have been enough to cue anyone in. But at that moment, Gabriel found himself unable to answer. Unable to relive it again—even for a moment.

Instead he leaned back against the wall, as tired as he'd ever been. A drip of blood slipped down Julian's cheek, and he shook his head with a broken sigh. "I'm sorry."

"It's fine." Julian shook his head dismissively, wiping the blood away without a second thought. "We came here to help you…" His dark eyes flickered

STARING AT THE FUTURE

around the ransacked apartment before coming up short. "I thought we'd come in time."

"You thought?" Gabriel repeated with a frown. "You didn't know?"

A strange tension flickered across his friend's face, and Gabriel suddenly understood. It appeared that Stryder's famous 'non-applicable tatù' had kept even the greatest psychic in the world at bay. Julian couldn't see his decisions. Not a single one. When those decisions happened to involve Gabriel, he couldn't see him either. His frustration at that fact had obviously been eating away at him, and Devon clapped him on the back before moving on.

"We came as soon as we could." He spoke in a quiet calm, discreetly scanning Gabriel up and down all the while. "As soon as Jules knew something was wrong."

"You decided to go to an outdoor market, and then everything went blank." A little crease formed between Julian's eyes as he tried to see past it even now. A few years ago, he might have taken something like that in stride. But the man standing in front of Gabriel now wasn't accustomed to anything in the world interfering with his sight. "No matter what I did, I couldn't see you. It was like you just vanished off the planet. I tried to call..."

Gabriel remembered the phone call he'd ignored. If only he hadn't. If only he'd used his head for once. Then maybe he would have run right home. And Natasha wouldn't be...

He bit down on his lip, forcing himself to go no further.

"There's a man here who's impervious to ink," he murmured, keeping his burning eyes fixed on the floor. "He was at the market. You wouldn't have been able to see."

The conversation lapsed into an uncharacteristic silence as two of the three men struggled to come up with something to say, while the third stared vacantly at the floor.

Oblivious to everything going on around him. Lost in his own little purgatory.

Devon's eyes flickered quickly around the room, performing the same initial assessment that Gabriel had done himself. They lingered on the tiny sundress, still in a pile in the center of the floor, before coming to rest on the broken pieces of the silver rose. "This man," he began tentatively, "the one Julian can't see—"

"Stryder," Gabriel interjected. His voice was raspy, as if he'd been shouting at the top of his lungs. "His name is Stryder."

Devon nodded slowly, throwing a quick glance at Julian before proceeding with a delicate sort of caution. "He took someone? Someone you... care about?"

Gabriel said nothing. He simply glared a burning hole in the floor.

The men exchanged another look, one that was hard to interpret. Probably because they were having trouble interpreting the situation themselves.

Over the years, they had seen no shortage of bloodshed and death. Kidnappings, murders, midnight car chases through rural Japan? They had braved it all, more times than they cared to admit. Braved it all and come out even stronger on the other side.

It wasn't the situation that was throwing them. It was Gabriel.

Since the first moment they'd met him all those years ago, he was the one member of the gang who could always be counted on to have a level head. To push immediately past the emotions or moral ambiguities of a situation, and fix his eyes on the target. Cromfield had driven it into his very bones, and he'd learned the lesson well. His focus was legendary. His resilience, unparalleled. As was his cold, almost callous, precision.

They'd teased him for it multiple times. Criticized him. Especially Devon. But they'd all leaned into it more times than they cared to admit. That unshakable calm had been their very salvation, and deep down they wouldn't have had it any other way.

They needed him like that. To provide a balance to their group. To provide that silent safety net, one they wouldn't hesitate in trusting with their lives.

That was Gabriel.

The man sitting in front of them...he was someone they'd never seen before.

Fortunately, they'd had training themselves. And the man they were dealing with wasn't just a friend. He had long since become a brother.

They stared for just a second more before branching off at the same time. Prioritizing their problems and working together as a team. While Julian gave Gabriel a cursory examination Devon began making a slow circle through the house, stopping every now and then to examine things that might be of interest. A broken mirror. A shattered mug. The five tiny claw marks ripped into the leather surface of the coffee table.

STARING AT THE FUTURE

His eyes tightened when he saw the table and he knelt silently, holding his own fingers up to the jagged tears. Determining the girl's approximate size. Determining her level of strength and consciousness as she was pulled, screaming, from the room. A second later he found the handkerchief, gave it the same cursory sniff as Gabriel, then dropped it in disgust.

"I'm fine, Jules," Gabriel muttered, pulling away as the psychic checked him over with practiced hands. "I wasn't here when it happened."

"No, but you've been getting into trouble since you left," Julian replied quietly.

Perhaps it was a good thing that the two men were fated to be brothers, because the soft-spoken psychic was the only person seemingly impervious to Gabriel's chilling stare. He ignored him completely, scanning for any damage before his hands suddenly went still.

"What's this?" He hesitated a moment, then pulled open the first few buttons on Gabriel's shirt. There was a soft gasp when he saw the fresh scar. The tiny bullet hole, just inches above his friend's heart. "*Gabriel.*"

His face paled in belated horror as Devon abandoned his search and came over to see it for himself. He, too, went still. Every muscle freezing at the same time.

"This is a nine-millimeter." He reached out instinctively, lightly running his fingers atop the scar. When he looked back up, he was pale as a sheet. "You got shot? Why didn't you call us? What the heck happened?!"

Gabriel shifted restlessly under their expectant stares, pulling away and buttoning up his shirt. He didn't have time for their sympathy, or the well-meaning reprimands that were sure to follow. In fact, he didn't have another second to lose.

"The same thing that happened in here." He pushed past Julian and swiftly made his way around the room, gathering up his things. "Stryder."

The men stared after him in amazement as his catatonic trance was suddenly abandoned, and he blurred into action. Slipping on his jacket, grabbing his cell phone off the floor, randomly straightening an overturned lamp.

"Come on. Now that you guys are here, we can start canvassing the neighborhood." If he didn't know where to start, then they were just going to have to do this old-school. Door to door in New York City. How long could it possibly take? "I'll take the west end. Julian, you can take the east. Devon, head south and we'll meet back—"

"Wait a second. Slow down." Devon stepped in front of him, inadvertently halting his perpetual motion. "You and I both know we're not going to get anywhere wandering around the neighborhood on foot. To start, Jules and I still don't even know who we're looking for. Why don't you just calm down, take a breath, and—"

"I'm not going to calm down!" Gabriel interrupted, depressingly aware that Devon's voice had taken on an instinctively soothing tone. The same tone he used on nervous witnesses and volatile assets. The tone that never failed to talk them down off the ledge. "And don't use that pandering voice with me, Devon. Don't talk to me like I'm someone else."

"I'm not." Devon took a step back, raising his hands. "I swear... I'm just saying—"

"Well, stop. There isn't time." Gabriel shoved past him towards the door, yanking it open with such force that the entire thing fell off its hinges and clattered to pieces in the middle of the floor. He looked at it for a second, at a total loss, before kicking the planks of wood to the side with the toe of his boot. "Doesn't matter," he muttered. "We'll fix it when we get back—"

"*Gabriel.*"

He didn't realize Julian was standing in front of him until he was staring deep into the psychic's eyes. Unlike Devon, he wasn't trying to calm or reason. He was neither wary nor anxious. He had no agenda whatsoever. He was simply sincere.

"This isn't helping her. We need to do something that's going to help."

Throughout the course of their training—either with Cromfield or at Guilder—everyone in the gang had picked up on certain tricks of the trade. Certain techniques and methods designed to help them gain a psychological edge. To turn the will of the subject in their favor. To silence a protestor, or agitate a crowd. To gain access to privileged information, or simply convince a person hell-bent on revenge to give up the ghost and go home.

As the years went by, they'd developed these skills even more. Adding layers of context and nuance. Tailor-fitting them to match each of their personalities.

Molly was pure emotion. Devon was persuasively calm. Angel scared people. Luke presented them with facts and raw data. Rae simply blew them all away. And Gabriel? Gabriel had been known to bend a rule or two to get what he wanted.

Yes, they all had their little tricks. All except Julian.

While he could lie just as well as the others, he didn't do it unless it was necessary. Instead, his approach was simple. He told people the truth. Even if it wasn't always easy. Even if it wasn't what they wanted to hear. The others had seen him move mountains with nothing more than quiet sincerity. In a way, it was the most effective method of all.

"She needs you," he said again softly. "Do this for her."

It was like dousing a flame. All at once, the fire that had suddenly propelled Gabriel cooled to a smoldering glow. Trapped in a holding pattern. Unable to stay, unable to leave.

He held his ground for a second more, his eyes drifting restlessly down the outer hallway towards the stairs, before he abruptly walked back inside. As there was no longer a door to slam he threw down his coat in frustration instead, gesturing impatiently at his friends.

"All right, then what?" he demanded. A part of him was aware he was misdirecting his rage at the last people who deserved it, but he was too far gone to care. At any rate, they didn't seem to mind. If anything, they seemed intensely relieved that he'd decided to stay. "I get what you're saying, but I'm not just going to sit around here and do *nothing*—"

"We're not going to do nothing," Devon said quickly, sinking carefully onto the couch. On the other side of the room, Julian did the same. "You're going to tell us everything that's happened, and then we're going to figure out a plan. Together."

That persuasive calm was back again, but this time Gabriel appreciated it. The same way he appreciated the strategic seating arrangements. He was now the only person left standing. It was a subtle move, but highly effective. One he'd done many times himself.

The last wave of resistance rushed out of him as he sank into the nearest chair with a weary sigh, running his hands through his hair. "I don't even know where to start..."

Devon bit his lip, debating whether to speak.

"Why don't you start with telling us what happened at St. Stephens?" Julian shot him a furious look, but he raised his hands defensively. "What? Like we *weren't* going to talk about it?" His eyes flickered curiously to Gabriel. "That was you, wasn't it?"

Gabriel glanced up in surprise, caught off guard by the question. A part of him wanted to instinctively deny it, but at this point the game was up. "Yeah...that was me."

"I knew it." Devon's eyes lit with triumph as Julian sullenly slapped a stack of bills into his waiting hand. "The second I heard the name of the church."

Gabriel shot them both a choice look, quoting their conversation from back in Iceland. "I thought you guys weren't keeping up with the BBC news..."

"We weren't." Julian's eyes flashed with sudden anger. "But when Angel calls *me* in the middle of the night, worried out of her mind, *I* always answer."

It was another reason the two men were well-suited. Aside from the aforementioned girl, Julian was one of the only people alive who could put Gabriel in his place.

He flushed again, bowing his head as the weight of the last few months settled hard upon his shoulders. Yes, he had effectively abandoned his friends and family. Yes, they had every right to be angry with him for that now.

But Julian wasn't particularly angry. Neither was Devon. They were simply concerned.

"St. Stephen's has been abandoned for years." Devon tilted his head curiously, studying Gabriel's face with interest. "Why now? What was so important about the church now?"

Gabriel paused a moment, staring between them. Both perched on the edge of their chairs. Both having just flown halfway around the world just to make sure he was all right. Both eternally sworn to do everything in their power to help him.

A feeling of actual relief rushed over him, paired with the faintest stirring of hope.

"It's not actually about the church," he answered suddenly, those endless months of walls coming down to let his family back inside. "It's about this book..."

Chapter 3

IT TOOK THE BETTER part of two hours to tell the rest of the story. Another hour after for Devon and Julian to pick through it with a series of unending questions. By the time they were finished the sun had risen over the tops of the distant skyscrapers, filling the room with a golden glow. The distant sound of pedestrians screaming foul profanities at passing taxi cabs filtered in as well.

"All that, and you didn't call..."

Devon had been unable to get past this one sticking point. He'd casually mentioned it the first time when Gabriel had found himself in jail. Brought it up again after the second encounter with Stryder, when he'd ended up getting shot. And hissed it vehemently through his teeth when Gabriel was attacked again in the subway, just a few days after that.

In his mind, it was incomprehensible. Unlike Gabriel, who had been programmed with the utter self-sufficiency of a lone agent, he had been trained with the idea of a team. An idea that hardened into stone when that team happened to become family. That family later went on to save the world, then set up a sort of neighborhood commune in residential London.

"I didn't call." Gabriel stretched his arms out in front of him, pushing to his feet to make his way once more towards the coffee. "Get over it."

Devon flashed him a hard look then deliberately poured the rest of the pot into his own mug, setting it back down with a smug clatter. "Not that it would have mattered if you did, as I was temporarily stranded in Iceland without a travel visa or passport."

Crap, I was wondering when he was going to bring that up.

"Why, what happened?" Gabriel asked innocently, stretching out his fingers as Devon's mug flew into his open hand. He tossed the metal spoon into the sink with a look of grave concern. "Did you lose your wallet?"

Devon didn't answer. He simply looked once between his old nemesis and the stolen coffee before turning sharply on his heel and heading back into the living room. Gabriel took a swig and followed him to the couch, the hint of a grin playing about his lips.

He may have been ingrained with an unyielding self-reliance, but he had latched onto the group dynamic far more than he was willing to admit. Just twenty-four hours ago, the world as he knew it had come to a screeching half. But now, after spending only a few hours in the company of his friends, he saw a light in the darkness. A little flicker of hope that would have been otherwise obscured. A few hours in, and he felt like he could breathe.

"You should be more careful with things like that," he continued sagely, "travelling in a foreign country and all." He downed the rest of the coffee with a smile. "Or better yet, if you find yourself in trouble, Devon, you should really just *call*."

He may love his family, but that didn't mean he didn't also love to antagonize them.

Devon opened his mouth for a scathing reply but at that moment Julian walked back into the room, inadvertently stopping the escalation before it could begin. His hair was still damp from a shower, and he cast a wistful glance at the empty coffee pot before settling down on the opposite couch. "You know there's no hot water, right?"

While Devon had caught a few hours of sleep on the flight over from Iceland Julian had stayed awake, trying in vain to break through Stryder's ink, blindly searching the future. As a result, his REM cycle was still trapped in the middle of the night, Reykjavik time. Fortunately, the Privy Council had programmed its agents to get by without the luxury of sleep.

Gabriel glanced over his shoulder to the bathroom, silently cursing the temperamental water-heater, before flashing a quick smile. "It'll help you stay awake. And speaking of..." He leaned forward, elbows on his knees. "What's the plan?"

He was too close to the situation to see it himself. Too far submerged to keep his head above water. His friends, however, had exactly the unbiased perspective that was required. It helped that they were also very, *very* good at their jobs.

"We need to go back to the restaurant where you were staying," Devon said briskly, slipping into a professional tone without realizing it. "Pull up the security feeds and see if we can find out what actually happened. If the fire spread as quickly as the news said, then Stryder couldn't have started it himself. Not without being seen. He had to have sent an agent instead. Which is actually kind of perfect for us."

Gabriel glanced at Julian, who finished Devon's assessment with a little nod. "If we can't track Stryder, we can track the agent. With any luck, he can lead us back to Natasha. Or at least point us in the right direction."

It was strange, hearing him say her name. Like he knew her. Like they could be friends. It was an abrupt collision of two worlds that Gabriel had never imagined intertwining. He liked it. "It's going to be hard getting in," Gabriel cautioned, remembering the crowd that had gathered the day before. "The whole place has been locked down by the police."

Devon considered this for a moment before his face lit up with a mischievous smile. "We'll just have to go as the police, then." He was on his feet the next second, pulling on his jacket as he headed to the door.

Gabriel stared after him for a moment before following suit—rolling his eyes all the while. "You PC kids and your penchant for playing dress-up has gotten out of control..."

"Uh, excuse me," Devon interjected sharply. "Weren't you the one who was pretending to be a PC kid yourself when we first met you?"

"Oh, no, that was all real," Gabriel replied smugly. "I was actually employed as an agent. Passed your little qualifying test and everything."

Devon shot him a pained look and disappeared into the hallway, while the other two gathered up their things. There was a thoughtful silence between them. One that Gabriel kept waiting for Julian to break. His friend wasn't one to pry, but there was only so long he could keep silent. Sure enough, a second before they made it to the door a hand shot out to catch his sleeve.

"Gabriel," Julian called softly, pulling him back a step as Devon went on ahead. His dark eyes sparkled inquisitively as he finally asked the question. "This girl...what is she to you?"

There was a moment of silence as Gabriel considered the question. He had been fully expecting it. All their hours of talking, all their endless analyses...and there was still one little detail they had yet to discuss. However, despite his anticipation, he still had no idea what to say.

Instead, his eyes flickered instinctively to the rose—still in silver pieces on the floor. Without seeming to think about it he raised his hand, resurrecting the broken shards and melding them back into some semblance of a whole. He stopped halfway through, and let them fall again. Shattering one by one as they fell back to earth.

What was the point? She was gone. There wasn't anyone to give it to.

"...she's someone I need to get back."

WHEN THEY LEFT THE apartment that morning, Gabriel was ready to go charging full-force across town. To take over the crime scene by force. To tear the city apart until the men who had wronged them were begging on their knees.

Unfortunately, they had a stop to make first.

"I don't believe it." Gabriel sat back in his chair, looking Devon up and down in open astonishment as he walked out of the changing room. "Just when I thought you couldn't look like more of an insufferable arse..."

Devon flashed him a sideways glare then straightened up in front of the mirror, turning this way and that. The three-piece suit clung to him like a second skin. Lending an automatic air of authority. An intimidating sort of confidence reflected in the instinctual deference shown by the other people in the store. All except Gabriel. He'd given his friends a ten-minute time limit to prepare for their little invasion, and at minute eight his patience was already up.

"Devon, just get the bloody suit already and let's leave." He slouched further down in his chair, shooting a look of disgust at the saleswomen who'd gathered discreetly to watch. "I can't believe we're out *shopping* anyway. Why didn't you just come prepared?"

Devon patiently ignored him, ripping off the tags attached to the clothes and handing them to a cashier along with a handful of bills. "You mean, why didn't I anticipate the need to infiltrate a crime scene before I left Iceland, and pack an Armani just in case? You're right," he adjusted his sleeves with a thoughtful frown, "how careless of me."

"Um...excuse me, sir?" Both men glanced over at the same time to see the cashier still hovering anxiously to the side, looking nervous to have interrupted. "We don't take cash."

STARING AT THE FUTURE

33

Devon blinked in surprise, then turned slowly to Gabriel. It was impossible to tell exactly which profanities were dancing behind his eyes, but Gabriel got the gist. He reached into his pocket with an innocent smile, then tossed a wallet through the air.

"I guess it's time this got back to you..."

"Are you sure?" Devon handed his card to the cashier with a dry smile. "I wouldn't want to inconvenience you."

"You mean any more than you already have?" Gabriel demanded, dropping his head back with a groan as the saleswomen swooned again. "Let's. Go."

"I'm paying now. Relax."

"Julian!" Gabriel turned his frustration to another target, absentmindedly unravelling a silk throw pillow into shreds. "Hurry up!"

The second changing room curtain pulled back and the psychic emerged, looking quite pleased with himself. He was wearing the same clothes as he had been that morning, with one simple accessory added on. One he seemed to feel made all the difference.

"Glasses?" Gabriel abandoned the pillow and pushed impatiently to his feet. "Really?"

Julian's smile faded slightly as he turned away from the mirror. "They make me look different. Help me get into character."

There was a beat.

"...really?"

Julian tucked them self-consciously into his shirt, just as Devon finished paying up front and cocked his head towards the door. "Done. And I got your ridiculous glasses, Jules. Let's go."

Together, the three men headed out of the store. Each one feeling a bit more deflated than when they'd walked in. Each one keeping it carefully to themselves. Gabriel knew, though. He knew how to read people. He'd spent a lifetime being trained to do so. The only thing about his friends was, they surprised him time and time again. He desperately hoped now was going to be another time for one of those surprises. They needed to find Natasha and kill Stryder.

The restaurant was only about twelve blocks away, and Gabriel found himself growing more and more nervous the closer they got. To start, he was hyperaware of the fact that they were heading back to the crime scene to do what he should've done in the first place. Get the security tape. Recover his belongings to avoid legal entanglements. Look for clues. Three things that had echoed loudly through Gabriel's head the last time he was there, but when presented with the nightmare head-on the only thing he'd done was freeze.

His hands started to twitch nervously as they neared a ten-block radius. By the time they reached block five, his heartbeat was pounding behind his eyes.

Fortunately, his friends were providing a welcome bit of distraction.

"Dev, look. They actually have hot dog vendors." Julian gestured to the side, looking absolutely delighted. "That's adorable. We should take a picture."

Devon glanced over, then helpfully slipped a quarter into an expired meter. "I just like their money. It looks so quaint."

Gabriel rolled his eyes. "Have you guys seriously never been to New York before?"

"Of course we have," Devon answered quickly, but his eyes were lit with curiosity as they flickered around the city street. "But only ever for work. And I've never been to Brooklyn."

"That's perfect," Gabriel muttered under his breath. "We're supposed to be blending in, yet here I am trapped with a man who would have delighted in being a meter maid, and another who sincerely believes if you wear glasses the world can't recognize the rest of your face."

Julian glanced down self-consciously at his brilliant costume, while Devon matched him stare for stare. "I'm sorry Jules and I have branched out our wardrobe to include things that didn't come from a hotel gift shop. Not everyone can pull off 'aspiring tennis pro' as well as you. But rest assured," he gestured to his clothes, "when the time comes this is going to work."

Gabriel wisely chose to keep his comments to himself. Not only did he not doubt his friend for an instant, but that 'time' was coming a lot sooner than he'd like.

The three friends came to an abrupt stop as the crowded sidewalk in front of them suddenly cleared, revealing the burnt-out ruins of Gabriel's first New York City home. The smell of burnt plastic and smoke still hung heavy in the air, and without thinking about it Gabriel took a tiny step back. His eyes tightened, and he pulled in a silent breath.

"Hey." All the teasing was gone as Devon turned to look him in the eye. The playful banter had morphed into something calm. Something steady. "You ready to do this?"

Before Gabriel could answer Julian clapped him gently on the shoulder, casually urging him forward at the same time. "This girl of yours…let's get her back."

It was the perfect thing to say. In a flash the new Gabriel was put away, and the old Gabriel made a sudden appearance. Cool. Confident. Collected. Ready for anything and everything the world could throw his way. He rolled back his shoulders with his signature poise and lifted his chin, his piercing green eyes fixed on the target.

"Let's do it."

SINCE CRASHING INTO his world uninvited, determined to steal the woman he loved, Gabriel had made it a point to make things as difficult for Devon Wardell as possible. He routinely sabotaged the man's attempts at a weekly date night. He spoiled his daughter with French chocolates and candy, dropping her back off at home where she proceeded to climb up the walls in a rabid sugar-high. He'd even gone so far as to cook Rae romantic candlelit dinners, pretending to be surprised when her angry husband stormed back through the door.

The subtle attacks had become more difficult once he and Devon became friends. It felt strange actively plotting against the man who went running with him every morning. He'd even gone so far as to leave the guy entirely alone each year on his anniversary. Granted, that was usually the day Gabriel stole his keys and took his newest car for a joy ride through the city.

But even Gabriel Alden had to admit there were things that Devon did well. Days when there was literally no one in the world he'd rather have by his side.

This was one of those days.

"James Augustus Wilbright, who exactly is in charge here?"

Devon strode into the middle of the crime scene without a second thought. Staring around as though he, himself, was the center of attention. Not the crumbling ruins of the diner.

"You!" He snapped his fingers impatiently, taking on a hint of a Southern drawl as he gestured the nearest officer forward. "What's your name, young man?"

Gabriel watched with wide eyes as the man in question stared in disbelief. He obviously had more than twenty years on this young upstart, but there was something about him that commanded authority. In the end, he couldn't help but reply.

"Officer Derrick Henneson. Seventy-Eighth Precinct." He paused suddenly, wondering why he was playing along. "And you are...?"

Instead of answering right away, Devon looked the man up and down. His lips parted at the sheer impertinence, and if Gabriel didn't know better he'd swear his friend was just a breath away from whipping out a pair of white gloves and slapping the man across the face. "Well, I told you once before, but I'll tell you again. You are speaking to James Augustus Wilbright." He threw out the name like some kind of Southern lord, gesticulating wildly enough to make Julian wince and Gabriel raise his eyebrows in disbelief. "FBI Crime Lab. Dallas." He reached into a pocket and flashed a badge too quickly for anyone to properly see it. If Gabriel had to guess, he'd say it was probably a London Polo Club membership card.

But no matter the circumstances, the words "FBI" were enough to get most anyone's attention. As was the badge. Even if the man in question sounded like he'd wandered off the set of *Gone with the Wind*, and was dressed like some Wall Street serial killer.

"FBI?" the officer stammered. "I didn't think this had reached that level of attention." He was about to say something else, when he suddenly paused, looking at Devon with borderline suspicion. "Why the Dallas branch?"

Devon leaned down with a sneer. "I'm not at liberty to disclose that information. Now why don't you run along and get your superior, before I start taking down some freakin' names!"

As if on cue, Julian stepped forward. Glancing impatiently down at his phone. Squinting, almost imperceptibly, against the useless prescription on his glasses. "What's the hold-up?"

STARING AT THE FUTURE

"That's just what I was wondering myself." Devon put his hands on his hips, spreading open the jacket of his newly purchased suit. "I do hope you have a good explanation, Officer Henneson. Seventy-Eighth Precinct."

Gabriel looked away with a grimace.

Holy moly, the man has a pocket watch.

"Yes, of course, I was just..." The poor officer trailed off again, staring at Julian with a bewildered frown. "Is he with the Bureau, too?"

Devon glanced at Julian with a look of supreme consideration before turning back to the man with a smirk. "He's my psychic."

There was a beat of silence, during which four pairs of eyes shot opposite directions.

Julian shot Devon a withering look, flashing the officer a tight smile. "It's an imprecise science..."

Officer Henneson absorbed this as best he could, floundering helplessly in the aftermath. "So, I'll just get my captain and tell him that James Augustus Wilbright and...his psychic are here to examine the crime scene?"

Devon's eyes narrowed as he brought himself up to his full height. "James Augustus Wilbright...the *Third*."

The man vanished without a trace. The three friends stared after him for a moment before Devon turned to the others, his British accent coming through loud and clear. "All right, well, that should buy us some time. I'll get the security feed. Gabriel, slip inside and grab whatever you might have left. Julian, look for clues."

Julian's face hardened as he walked past Devon into the restaurant, knocking him hard in the shoulder in the process. "...your *psychic*?"

Devon's lips twitched up with a faint grin. "Be sure to lay your hands on things, and chant in tongues. They love that kind of stuff."

Gabriel stared at him for a long moment before he flicked the chain of the pocket watch and walked away muttering. "What did I say about dress-up..."

It wasn't any easier, walking around the burnt-out remains of the restaurant, but it was at least manageable now that Gabriel had people in his corner. He moved quickly through the crowd of police, already far fewer than had come the day before—frowning all the while, as if he, too, had somewhere legitimate to be. To bolster his story, he grabbed a discarded NYC Police Academy windbreaker, slipping it over his shoulders as he headed down the scorched hallway to his room in the back.

It was remarkable. The rest of the place was in ruins, but Gabriel's room looked like it hadn't even been touched. His bed was still messy and un-made—just the way he'd left it—and his black bag of clothes was still half-wedged under a loose floorboard in the corner.

How did they explain it to themselves, he wondered as he moved quickly across the room and picked up his things. Fortunately, he'd had his wallet on him, and there was nothing inside to provide identification should anyone have already stumbled across it. If he'd left it, Devon would be a suspect. Too bad he'd tossed it back to his buddy, otherwise he'd have dropped it under the bed. Didn't matter now. *How'd they rationalize the fact that in this run-of-the-mill electrical fire, one room was completely undisturbed?*

Another cursory sweep of the room, and his eyes fell on the empty aquarium.

And what the heck happened to my fish?

Deciding that was a mystery for another day, he darted quickly into the bathroom to gather whatever things he might have left. He paused at the sink for a moment, his hands lingering over Magda's hairbrush. There was a split second of hesitation before he picked that up as well and slipped it into his bag.

By the time he got outside Julian had already joined Devon, and Devon was putting on the second half of his show. This time, to the man who was really in charge.

"Just what exactly do you mean," he drawled impatiently, a hint of British frustration leaking through, "the restaurant was on a separate security grid from the rest of the street?"

The captain wrung his hands nervously as he fidgeted and twitched under Devon's unrelenting glare. "It was completely separate," he clarified quickly. "It was on both. A private system, newly installed, and the same public grid as the rest of the block."

Gabriel froze in his tracks, his face growing suddenly pale. Why hadn't he put it together before? The day before the place burned down, Peter and Magda had a brand-new security system installed! They'd been chattering about it for almost a week, but he hadn't even noticed.

"And what about the cameras on the rest of the street?" Devon pressed. "You're telling me that they all went down at the same time? A city-wide blackout? No explanation?"

"No, sir. They didn't all go down," the captain answered anxiously. "Just...just every camera on this particular block."

Devon raised his eyebrows slowly, sending a collective shiver through the rest of the block. "Just every camera...on *this* block."

Gabriel saw where he was going at the last minute. Understood the problem just a second after his friend's voice rang out through the air. Devon was searching for a conspiracy. Incompetence. Anything that could explain the sudden blackout. But Gabriel knew better.

He happened to know that the cameras had gone down long before the fire. "I think we can excuse that for now," he interjected quietly, coming to stand by Devon's side. "But we're going to need to see the private tapes."

Devon glanced over in surprise as the rest of the officers looked him up and down. He'd had the good sense to ditch the police windbreaker, but they still had no idea who this upstart was or why in the world he was in a place to be making demands.

There was an awkward pause, but Devon recovered himself quickly. "Of course we will, Marcus. Go wait in the car." He waved casually to the sidewalk behind him, then held out his hand. "And yes, Captain, I will need those tapes."

For one of the first times, Gabriel did as he was told. He left the strange scene behind him and headed out to the street. But on the way, he grabbed a police radio. And his bag. And a gun.

"WHAT THE HECK WERE you doing?" Devon demanded the second he rounded the corner and saw Gabriel and Julian waiting beside a parked cab. "I was going to get the tapes, Gabriel. You didn't have to—"

"Stryder's men took out the cameras on the street," Gabriel interrupted. Both men turned to him in surprise, and he nodded slowly. "It's the reason they were able to convince the Fischers to upgrade to a private system. A system I'm assuming they installed themselves. If you had pressed the captain to look into the original outage, there's a chance you could have risked exposing whatever ink Stryder employed to get the job done. At any rate, we can get what we need from the private tapes. There's no need to acquire the others."

He waited patiently as the others absorbed this and got quickly on board. For the first time in what felt like ages, he felt like his old self. Steady. Calm. Perpetually moving forward. A tangle of emotions was still raging beneath the surface, but for the time being it was carefully held at bay. Giving him the clarity of thought he needed to get the job done.

"On that note," he continued, turning to his friends, "Julian, do you have a camera?"

"Yeah." Julian rifled around in his bag, extracting something that looked as though it had been recently stolen from the New York City Police Department. He flashed Devon a quick look as he pulled out the security feed and fitted the chip inside. "I picked it up while you were busy playing the hero of Savannah..."

A faint grin flitted up the side of Gabriel's face as the camera clicked on, but faded the second the picture loaded onto the screen. He was right. The new security system had been Stryder's people all along. He was a fool not to have seen it before. "That's Peter and Magda," he said quietly, shifting for a better view. "The morning of the seventh. This had to be right before the fire."

The sudden realization of what he was about to see hit hard and he sucked in a quick breath, bracing himself breathlessly against the stone. Devon flashed him a quick look, and Julian looked up nervously, as though wondering if he should shield the camera.

"Gabriel," he began hesitantly, "you don't need to see this. Dev and I can—"

"Be quiet," Gabriel commanded softly, "it's starting."

The door to the restaurant opened, and a strange man walked through the door. He was of medium build and frame, not overtly threatening, but there was something about the way he carried himself that made Gabriel's blood run cold. This man knew exactly what he was capable of. Furthermore, the rest of them were about to find out.

He talked briefly with the unsuspecting couple, keeping his face angled instinctively away from the cameras. There was no sound, but it soon became clear by everyone's body language that something was going very wrong. Magda gestured to the back and shook her head, whilst Peter came to stand in front of her, folding his arms across his chest.

It didn't matter. There was nothing they could have possibly done.

STARING AT THE FUTURE

One minute the man was standing in front of them. The next, he was gone. Gabriel watched with wide-eyes as he reappeared in front of Peter, hardly glancing up as he slipped a knife deep inside his chest. Magda threw open her mouth in a scream, but before she could take a step the man was behind her as well, thrusting the same knife into her spine.

A glass vase was quickly shattered, its pieces scattered precariously around the room. A second later, a host of plates and glasses were soon to follow. With a careless boot, the man kicked the couple down onto the wreckage, a plausible cause for their wounds.

He didn't stop to enjoy his work; he was nothing but business. There were a few seconds where he was off-frame, assumedly ripping through the electrical system and planting some sort of incendiary device, but when he was striding back into the main room he suddenly paused.

There was a split second where he stood perfectly still, then he raised his eyes to the camera with a little smile. Gabriel's blood boiled in his veins as he leaned a few inches closer, his eyes burning a hole in the screen. The man stood there a moment longer, then lifted his hand with a little wave. A second later, he was gone.

Just before the place went up in flames. Just before the sweet couple who'd taken Gabriel in with just the kindness of their hearts, slumped lifelessly onto the bloody floor.

The image went suddenly dead. Obscured in black-and-white static. Julian flipped the camera off, and for a moment the three men stood there in silence.

A teleporter. How can we catch a teleporter?

Gabriel had only ever met one. It had taken Cromfield's entire team just to track the guy down, and even then, they were unable to lay a hand on him. In the end, they simply waited for him to exhaust himself before Cromfield went inside and did the job himself.

It's impossible. There's just no way that we can...

But even as he thought the words, Gabriel suddenly stopped himself. His eyes flickered to the men standing beside him, and for possibly the first time in his life he said a little prayer of thanks. Out of all the people in the world, he couldn't imagine a better trio for this particular task. Who better to catch a teleporter than the exact people who'd flown out to help?

Someone who could see him coming. Someone who was fast enough to catch him.

Someone who wouldn't hesitate to pull the trigger.

Chapter 4

"IT HAD TO BE A TELEPORTER."

Devon popped open the lids to three more beers and added them to the horde of empty ones already on the table. The three men had been sitting in Natasha's dilapidated living room for the better part of three hours, but were still no closer to a solution than when they'd sat down.

Gabriel shook his head. The alcohol might have made his friends fuzzy, but his head was clear. "There has to be a way. Julian, can't you get any sort of read on him?" They were wasting time drinking, yet what else could they do but wait? Wait for a plan. Wait for news. Wait for what?

Julian leaned back in his chair, lifting the beer to his lips with a frustration he made no effort to hide. "I can tell you that a few minutes ago, he was at a coffee shop in Queens. A few minutes before that, he was at a hardware store in Brooklyn. And a few minutes before that, he was on a street somewhere on the Upper East Side."

It was twice now that his legendary ink had been thwarted by unsavory characters hiding in what he and Devon still considered 'the colonies.' He was starting to take it personally. The fact that he was on his sixth beer in less than an hour didn't help.

"But isn't there a way that you can get a step ahead and figure out where he's planning to go *next*?" Gabriel pressed. "You know...almost like you're *predicting the future*?"

Julian flashed him a cold look, but as much as he'd like to throw down the winning point it wasn't an answer he was able to give. "I *would*, except there's next to no pre-meditated thought. The guy doesn't really think before teleporting. He just does it."

Devon set down his drink and leaned forward, resting his elbows on his knees. "Well, maybe we can narrow it down. Maybe he follows some sort of a pattern—"

"Devon, I kid you not, about twenty seconds ago I could swear the guy was somewhere in Germany." Julian shook his head slowly, draining the second half of his drink. "If there's a way to find this guy, it isn't by watching his future."

The words lent an uncharacteristic air of discouragement to the proceedings, and the men fell silent once more. Each one lost in thought. It wasn't often they came up against an enemy they weren't unable to outmaneuver. Let alone when they were working together. It was like, no matter what they did Stryder was three steps ahead. Hiding in a murky, unknown future.

"What about Angel?" Gabriel asked suddenly. The others exchanged a quick look that was lost in his sudden burst of excitement. "Jules, you can see when he stops moving for the night, and she can just freeze the entire city block. He won't be able to—"

"Angel's not flying out here," Julian said shortly.

Gabriel paused mid-sentence, staring back in disbelief. His eyes flickered to Devon, only to find him staring determinedly at the floor. "Why not? It's a *great* idea. She'll be able to—"

"And what's going to happen to Natasha in the meantime?" Devon cut in swiftly. Julian shot him a quick look of gratitude, one that was also lost on the third member of their group. "If we're going to make a play to get her back, then we don't have any time to waste."

No time to waste? Drinking beer wasn't wasting time? Gabriel wanted to argue, wanted to protest and pull out his phone, summoning his little sister to the heart of Brooklyn where she could work her twisted spell on whoever was getting in his way. But Devon's words touched a dark place in his heart.

He was right. There was no time to waste.

"So, then, where does that leave us?" Gabriel's fingers balled up into helpless fists as his foot tapped an impatient rhythm. "Without the teleporter, we don't have—"

A sudden knock on the door and the entire room froze.

Another knock, and the three of them sprang to attention.

"Natasha!" a loud voice called from the other side. A voice that was clumsy with drink and strangely familiar. "Tash, you get your butt out here! Right now!"

STARING AT THE FUTURE

Julian's eyes flashed instinctively white. Devon stiffened in alarm, gazing cautiously at the door before shooting Gabriel a tense look. "Friend of yours?" he mouthed.

Gabriel shook his head and took a step forward, his eyes fixed on the fractured frame. A few more strong knocks and the thing would break apart in pieces. As it stood, the only things holding it up were a few crooked nails and a prayer.

"NATASHA!"

The voice was angrier now. More insistent. Exactly the way Gabriel had imagined it merely by looking at the constant shadow of fear in the back of Natasha's eyes.

He wasn't going to let him in. He'd made the decision almost immediately. The man might have some familial claim to her, but he wasn't stepping over the threshold.

Unfortunately, Gabriel hadn't counted on the fact that the man might have a key...

There was a metallic scrape in the doorknob and he took a sudden step back, his green eyes flickering briefly around the ransacked apartment. Three men, a trashed flat, and a missing stepdaughter. What kinds of conclusions was the guy going to make?

A second later, Gabriel decided he didn't care.

"WHERE THE..."

The man was everything he'd imagined, and so much more. Thick, portly belly. Small, beady eyes. A scruffy beard that didn't entirely hide the tobacco stains smeared around his mouth. And a temper. Gabriel could see the temper all the way across the room.

He'd pulled up short, surprised to find not his stepdaughter but a trio of tall, good-looking men standing in the living room instead. Anger gave way to surprise. Which gave way to suspicion. Which turned back into anger before the door had even swung shut.

"Who are you?" he demanded. "Where's Natasha?!"

The other two glanced at Gabriel for their cues. They had no idea who the man was. For all they knew, the two of them were already acquainted. But a flicker of worry was troubling Julian's eyes. One that hadn't been there before he'd glanced into the future.

After a second of consideration, Gabriel stepped forward. As careless and unconcerned as if he dealt with raging stepfathers every day. "She's out," he said shortly. "Go home."

Bold words. As rude as they were insulting. No explanation was given. No conjecture as to when she might return. The hint of an actual smile pulled up the corners of Gabriel's mouth as the man's eyes widened in surprise. A second later, a vein started pulsing in the side of his neck.

"She's *out?*" he quoted dangerously, sending out a spray of spit from between his bared teeth. "I can see that she's out. She didn't come home last night. Where the hell is she?"

Devon and Julian glanced at the back of Gabriel's head but said not a word as he took another step forward, projecting an infuriating air of unshakable calm. "Like I said. *Out.* I suggest you come back at a better time."

By now, the man's face had turned a furious shade of puce. That pulsing vein was likely to explode. "And who are you?" he snarled, looking Gabriel up and down. "Her pimp?"

Gabriel's fingers twitched and Devon stepped quickly in between, providing an intentional buffer between the two men. "Natasha left this morning to visit a friend in Queens, said she'd probably be gone a few days. If you like, we'd be happy to take a message."

There was that tone again. The one designed to ease tensions. Unfortunately, given the two men in question, Devon didn't have a chance.

The man finally tore his eyes away from Gabriel, and seemed to notice the other two men the very first time. His eyes widened for a moment and his mouth went slack, staring in open disbelief at Devon's four- thousand-dollar suit. A moment later, he put two and two together. "You're not her pimp...you're her dealer."

That calming façade melted away for a moment as Devon's mouth fell open in honest surprise. "Excuse me?"

"What's she on?" he growled. "Smack? Meth?"

"Sir, I swear to you, there's nothing—"

"How do you even have a key?" Gabriel interrupted suddenly. The room went dead quiet as three pairs of eyes turned his way. "Does she know you have it?"

STARING AT THE FUTURE

There was a split-second pause then the man stormed across the room, not stopping until he was standing just a few inches away from Gabriel's face. "Do you have any idea who I am?! I'm the man who pays for this little crap-hole! I'm Natasha's *only living family*! The person who takes care of her!" His beady eyes flashed as he stretched up on his toes with a menacing sneer. "Who are *you*?!"

A flash of anger shot through Gabriel's eyes, but it quickly simmered down into a chilling smile. "I'm the man who knows better."

You could have heard a pin drop. Even the incessant street traffic came to a momentary pause as the men faced off against each other. Neither one giving an inch of ground.

"The person who takes care of her?" Gabriel continued in that soft, deadly voice. "You're the chain around her neck. A vibrant young girl tethered to a miserable drunk. You don't give a crap about Natasha. You just want to keep someone else in that house, so that when you eventually pass out in a pool of your own vomit choking on your last breath, it won't be the neighbor's dog that finds you. It will be the only person left on earth who will remember your miserable name. If only for a time."

The room was dead still. Poised on the edge of a knife. For a second, it looked like things could have gone either way. Then a flash of fear flickered across the man's face.

He took a small step back. Shaken, but not yet defeated.

"Tell Natasha...tell Natasha that if I ever see you in this place again, not only will I stop sending the rent payments but she can find herself a different place to live."

Gabriel's face betrayed not a hint of emotion as he slowly looked the man up and down.

A latent memory floated suddenly to the surface. One of him and Natasha walking back home after having dinner with Canary in Brooklyn. She'd warned him that the old woman was never going to back down. That once she saw a specter of danger hanging over his head, she'd make it her personal mission to forever keep him safe.

"What about you?" he'd asked. "She ever see a specter over you?" He remembered the way her eyes had hardened. Remembered the hunched tightening of her tiny shoulders as she gazed unblinkingly into the dark horizon. "She always sees a specter over me..."

He said the words without thinking. Without, for a second, considering them himself.

"Natasha's not going to live with you anymore. She's coming to live with me."

There was a soft intake of breath somewhere behind him. A feeling of total astonishment that permeated the room. A sudden chill swept over his shoulders, raising the hairs on the back of his neck as the ramifications of what he'd just done began to slowly sink in.

Oh crap. Crap, crap, crap crap, crap...

"She is?" the stepfather asked in disbelief.

"She is?" Julian echoed softly, just as thrown off balance as the rest.

She ISN'T. What am I saying?! She ISN'T.

...unless she wants to?

Gabriel pulled in a deep breath and raised his chin, squaring his shoulders as he looked the man right in the eye. "She is. And I'll be taking over the payment on this place. In short, your presence is no longer necessary. You can go."

It wasn't an offer so much as a frightening command.

The man's eyes slowly travelled down Gabriel's muscular arms, all the way to his ready fists, before he gulped silently and took a tiny step towards the door. "Don't think there's any coming back from this." He breathed heavily through his nose, groping blindly behind him for the knob. "If she walks away from me, there isn't ever any coming back! Do you understand?!"

Gabriel only smiled. "Careful. That's a tricky door."

The thing shattered into pieces as the man stormed out into the hall, falling in jagged shards out of the frame. He paused for a moment, flinching at the sound, then strode off towards the elevator, never to be seen or heard from again.

Devon stepped out into the hall, making sure that he was gone before turning back with a rather mild expression. "Well...I guess that's one way to have handled the situation." His eyes flickered to Gabriel with the hint of a smile before turning to Julian. "What do you say, Jules? I knew it was a doomed cause just from the look on your face after you checked the future."

Julian shook his head slowly, a bemused smile settling across his face. "Actually, I saw Gabriel reaching out and strangling the man. So, I guess we should

STARING AT THE FUTURE

be grateful for at least some semblance of a rational response. Plus, Gabriel got a roommate out of it, so..."

The two of them turned with matching grins, but Gabriel was still staring at the exact place the stepfather had vanished through the open door, lost in thought. A look of dawning realization lit up his eyes as he murmured, almost to himself, "People go back to what they know. That's why Natasha kept going back to the house in Brooklyn, again and again. People go back to what they know..."

Devon and Julian shared a quick look, but before either one of them could ask the question Gabriel pulled out of his trance with a sudden gasp.

"I know how we can find the teleporter."

Chapter 5

"YOU SAID IT YOURSELF, Julian." Gabriel took long strides down the city street, hardly noticing that the others were having trouble keeping up. "We're not going to find this guy by watching his future. So, forget the future. Maybe we find him by looking into his past..."

Julian dodged a crowd of angry tourists, wincing apologetically as he trailed in his friend's wake. "Yeah, but you know that's not exactly my specialty, right? Or yours, or Dev's."

"Where are we going, anyway?" Devon quickly righted a display booth of jewelry that Gabriel had knocked over in his hurry to get to the next block. "We don't even know the guy's name. For all we know, he could be..." He trailed off suddenly, almost running into Gabriel when he came to an abrupt stop. "A park? You think we're going to find him in a park?"

Gabriel pulled in a deep breath of the open air, smiling as the aroma of trees and freshly cut grass washed over him. "We didn't go to the park for him. We came here for your wife."

Devon froze where he stood, hardly noticing the cab that screeched to a stop just inches away from hitting him. "I'm sorry...did you say my *wife*? What does Rae have to do with anything—"

"We didn't want to video chat with her in the middle of a raided apartment." Gabriel settled down on a bench beneath the trees and pulled out his phone. "She'd worry. This way, it looks as though we're all enjoying a lovely afternoon outside. Nothing more than that."

"Why are we video chatting at all?" Devon demanded, using his tatù to grab the phone out of Gabriel's hands before he could dial. "She's half a world away, and I didn't...I didn't exactly tell her that Jules and I were making a stop on our way back from Iceland."

"You didn't?" Julian exclaimed. He took one look at his friend's miserable face, then burst out laughing. "Dude, you're an idiot."

STARING AT THE FUTURE

"And what was I supposed to tell her?" Devon held the phone out of reach as Gabriel made an impatient swipe for it. "That we were boarding a flight back to London, when you saw Gabriel suddenly disappear off the face of the planet? When she was home alone with Aria? You wanted me to call up and tell her that?"

"No, I'm actually glad you did what you did." Julian settled himself on the bench with a cheerful smile. "This way, I get to see what she's going to do to you."

Devon bowed his head with a little groan, but surrendered the phone when Gabriel reached for it again. He perched on the table behind the bench, half-shielded by his friends.

It didn't take long for Rae to answer. She picked up on the first ring.

"Gabriel!" Her face lit up with an automatic smile, creating a gorgeous glow around her as she moved about the kitchen. In London, the sun was just beginning to set, and Aria was already set up in her booster chair awaiting her dinner. "This is a surprise!"

A wave of instinctual relief swept over Gabriel, and his face relaxed into a genuine smile. One that only brightened when Aria waved at him, her little fingers covered in food. "A surprise for me, too, love. I don't want to take up much of your time." He held out his hand and Julian handed off the camera he'd stolen from the crime scene, already cued up with the teleporter's face splashed across the front. "I just need a quick favor." He held up the picture to his phone, letting her get a good look at the picture. "This man...can you tell me a bit about him? Places he might be? People he might have left behind?"

She paused mid-step, still holding a pot of macaroni and cheese that she was in the process of giving to her daughter. "Use Carter's tatù, you mean? Just based on a picture?" Her eyes tightened with worry. "That's a bit of a stretch..."

Gabriel sighed and bowed his head, nodding all the while. He seemed to be hearing that a lot lately. But what was the point in having super-friends if you didn't make impossible demands on them every once in a while?

"I can try," she said quickly, eager to help whatever way she could. "I'm just saying, I'm not sure whether or not it will..." She paused suddenly, squinting at the screen. "Wait a second, is that Julian's jacket?"

Julian sucked in a quiet breath, and discreetly edged away.

"And Devon's wedding ring!" she exclaimed, pointing indignantly at the screen. "I see it there behind you! What's going on? You guys are all together?!"

Her frustration was almost palpable, and Devon leaned apologetically into the frame. It would have been better if he and Julian had simply stayed out of the shot altogether, but while they weren't eager to volunteer their presence they were too afraid of her to hide it outright. "Hey, babe." He tried his best for a smile. "Jules and I took a little detour..."

"A little detour to New York?!" she demanded. "I recognize that statue behind you. You guys are in Brooklyn, right? That's Fort Greene Park!"

Devon flinched and Julian turned his head to the side, speaking under his breath. "I always forget that she's actually from here—"

"Hey, genius! Super-hearing, remember?" she interrupted loudly, rewarding each of them with an icy glare. "So, what's so important in New York that you guys decided to fly halfway around the world and have a picnic in the park...*without calling your wife*?"

"This man," Gabriel said again, circling her back on point while Devon and Julian cringed behind him. "What can you tell me about him?"

With a look of intense exasperation that scarcely hid her smile, she set down the noodles and held the picture up to her face, her blue eyes dilated with concentration. As little Aria danced and squealed in the background, throwing her dinner all over the walls, Rae slipped into a sort of trance. At one point she actually reached out her fingers to touch the screen. "It doesn't really work when it's not in person," she murmured, tilting her head to the side as she continued to try. "I can't get a good read on him, none of the specific memories and details of his life...but there *is* something weighing on him. Occupying his every thought."

Gabriel's breath caught in his chest, but he kept his voice steady. "What is it?"

For a moment those blue eyes glassed over completely, gazing out into worlds and memories the rest of them would never know. Then she shook herself back to the present. "His girlfriend left him. Moved out of the city. Just a few days ago." Her breath was quick, and the sentences were short and choppy as she tried to regain her equilibrium. "It's all he's thinking about. The place they used to share in the Bronx."

STARING AT THE FUTURE

At that point Julian leaned suddenly forward, staring at the camera with a thoughtful frown. "Is it a loft? No real furniture. Just a table, and a mattress pushed up against the wall?"

Gabriel glanced quickly between them as Rae nodded slowly. "That's the one." Her lovely face screwed up in a sudden apology. "I can't tell where it is, but—"

"No need," Devon said quickly, pulling a paper and pencil out of his jacket pocket and handing them to Julian. "Draw it for me. I'll upload it into the database and see what comes up."

As Julian's hand began flying over the page, Gabriel let out a silent sigh of relief and turned back to the camera with a gentle smile. "Thanks, gorgeous. You're the best."

It never ceased to amaze him, the profound effect his family could have. Just the sound of their voices, a fleeting smile...he suddenly felt unbearably homesick.

"I am, aren't I?" Rae flipped back her hair with a grin, one that faded the longer she looked at the screen. "So, is anyone going to tell me who this guy is? Or what exactly you're going to do once you find him?"

Gabriel stiffened but Devon leaned forward with an easy smile, pushing him aside to get some screen-time with his wife. "We're going to ask him a few questions is all. A few quick questions, then Jules and I will come home. No big deal."

Rae's eyebrows lifted slowly, and she shook her head with a grin. "Honey, you know that you're the *worst* liar in the entire world, right?"

Devon opened his mouth to respond, but Julian swiftly interrupted. "It's true. None of us have any idea how it was that you became a spy."

Before the argument could progress any further, there was a little giggle as Aria hurled her plate of cheesy noodles at the microwave clock with shocking precision.

"Daddy, look!" she trilled happily. "Did you see?"

Devon leaned forward with a smile, easing the phone out of Gabriel's hands. "I sure did, you little champion! That was an awesome throw!" His smile faded a bit when Rae shot him a sharp look. "I mean...don't throw your food, Arie-bug. Your mother worked hard on that." In an undertone, he couldn't help but add, "Rae, you didn't conjure it, did you? I mean, if you did, she was only protecting herself—"

"No, I did not." Rae bristled defensively, waving the empty box. The girl could harness the powers of the universe, but Heaven forbid she try to make a simple plate of food. "But, for the record, I think you've all blown my attempts at cooking *way* out of proportion."

The men shook their heads in unison. Behind Rae's back, Aria was shaking her head as well. Gabriel flashed her a secret wink, prompting her to fling one more noodle before he turned back to her mother with a little grin.

"Well, we've got to run, my dear. But like Devon said, nothing to worry about. A quick trip to the Bronx, and I'll send your husband straight back to you. Probably still in one piece."

Rae shrugged as if she couldn't care less one way or another. Only someone who knew her very well could see the flicker of concern. "However many pieces you can manage."

"I'll see you soon, love." Devon winked at the camera. "Promise."

A very reluctant smile tugged at the corners of her lips.

"See that you do."

The line went dead, just as there was a sudden beep from Devon's phone. He pulled the download up immediately, scanning briefly over the blueprints before flashing them at Julian.

"Is this the place you saw?"

Julian frowned for a moment at the image, and nodded his head. "Yeah, it's the same size and layout. Definitely the right building, and I saw him go there at least five times yesterday. I'm not sure what floor he's on, but I should be able to tell by the view outside the window."

"Perfect." Gabriel pushed swiftly to his feet. "Then let's get going."

The other two stayed right where they were, staring up at him with a mixture of shock, amusement, and utter exasperation.

"You don't think we should make a plan first?" Devon asked quizzically, surveying his friend with a little grin. "Before we go racing in there, guns drawn?"

Gabriel didn't wait for them to catch up. Nor did he look where he was going as he headed straight across the street and down into the subway. "I have a plan," he murmured, moving farther and farther into the tunnel as the sun gave way to darkness. "Catch the freakin' teleporter."

ABOUT FORTY MINUTES later, the three men were standing on a street corner in the middle of the Bronx—staring up at the same sun-drenched building.

"So how exactly did you happen to stumble into the only ring of inked criminals in all of New York City?" Devon muttered, squinting his eyes against the bright afternoon light. "Or is it some kind of cave-born magnetism? You couldn't physically stay away."

Julian shoved him with a grin but Gabriel kept his eyes on the target, staring up at the seven levels of apartments, wondering which one their teleporter was squatting in. "Just lucky, I guess." A sudden movement caught his eye, and he tugged Julian a step forward. "There. Fourth floor. Could that be it?"

Julian's eyes glassed over, and he shook his head. "No, that's a little too high. I'd guess he's either on the second or—*wait*!" For a split second he froze, his dark eyes clouding over with prophetic white. When he came out of it a moment later, he was a different man. "He's here. Third floor. Corner flat. Facing southeast."

All at once the three young friends disappeared, taking their banter and jokes with them. What remained were three seasoned spies. Three young men trained to the highest levels of proficiency. Each one ready to do whatever it took to get the job done.

"We go in all at once," Devon muttered under his breath, "catch him by surprise. Chances are we're only getting one shot at this. If the man disappears, he won't come back here again."

There was a moment of silence, then they walked forward at the same time. Moving with an ingrained synchronicity. A predatory efficiency. Like lions on the hunt.

The double-deadbolt crumbled in Devon's hand, and the three friends slipped silently inside the building. There wasn't an elevator so they ghosted up the stairs, taking careful stock of their surroundings all the while. It took no time whatsoever to find the right apartment, and as they came to a stop in front of the door they were able to hear movement on the other side.

This is it. Gabriel's muscles tightened at the ready as Natasha's lovely face drifted through his mind. *Time to bring you home.*

The gang moved like a pack. Each falling effortlessly into his role.

As Gabriel kicked down the door Devon streaked inside, nothing more than a blur of color. The bits of dust and plaster were still falling from the frame as Julian and Gabriel leapt over the threshold, each one aiming a steady-handed weapon into opposite corners of the room.

It was a beautiful attack. One that would have made even Carter proud.

Unfortunately...it failed to impress their teleporter.

"'Bout time you all showed up." The three men looked up slowly to see the man in question perched atop a tall grandfather clock, his legs dangling down either side as he chewed noisily on a sandwich. "Guess the PC has started hiring based on looks, not talent."

He had a strong Cockney accent. Obviously a transplant who'd fled England in the wake of Cromfield's demise. There was a large scar running up the side of his face, and Gabriel wondered if he'd fought in the battle at the sugar factory. Of all the inked traitors they'd taken prisoner, this man would have had a built-in escape.

Devon had neither the time nor the patience to answer his taunts. Instead, he streaked towards the clock, moving faster than anyone in the room could see.

Except...the teleporter was faster.

There was no fluidity to what he did. No pattern of movement. One second, he was sitting there. The next, he was just gone.

"Looking for me?"

The men whirled around once more to see him reclining peacefully in a rocker pushed against the far wall of the room. He was still eating his sandwich, and when he saw Devon by the clock he flashed him a roast-beef grin. "Nice try, fox. But you'll have to be faster than that."

While Devon looked more than up to the challenge, it was Gabriel who made the next move. His fingers spread open in his sleeve, searching for the iron in the man's blood, but no sooner had he secured a grip than there was another *pop* and the guy vanished into thin air.

STARING AT THE FUTURE

"Up here." The gang whirled around yet again, only to find him perched atop a rickety old chair. The sandwich was gone, and by now it was easy to see he was clearly enjoying himself. "So, this is it, huh? The Privy Council's best and brightest." He looked them up and down with a toothy smile. "I have to say, I'm a little disappointed."

There was another *pop*, and before the gang knew what was happening the man was slamming Julian's head into the cinderblock wall. The psychic fell to his knees with a soft cry, blinking back a wave of blood that was pouring into his dark eyes.

"No looking into the future now," the teleporter chided softly, his smile fading for the first time. "If you guys want me, you'll have to take me down fair and square."

He vanished again before Gabriel had a chance to grab him. Before Devon had even finished helping Julian back onto his feet.

"Fair and square?" Devon called angrily, his bright eyes flashing around the room as he waited for the man to reappear. "How about you stay still for one second, and we'll see—"

"I didn't come here for you," Gabriel interrupted, walking slowly to the center of the room, hands held innocently at his sides. "I only came here for Natasha. Where are they keeping her? Tell me...and we'll walk right back out of here. Never to come back again."

There was nothing but silence. No man. No sound. But, even though they couldn't see him, Gabriel had no doubt that the three of them were continuously being watched.

"Or..." he rotated slowly on the spot, letting his voice ring out in all four corners of the room, "...we could keep tracking you down. We could keep showing up at your house. At your work. Wherever we can find you. And one day, you might not be so lucky. One day, you might just find that you weren't quite fast enough—"

There was a sudden *pop* in the air behind him, and Gabriel whirled around just in time to get kicked across the face. Devon shouted something he couldn't make out, but by the time his eyes snapped open the man was gone again.

A rush of blinding pain shot through his body and he gritted his teeth to keep quiet, blinking the stars from his eyes as he pushed stiffly to his feet.

"Or we could just kill you right now..."

The ghost of a chuckle echoed through the air before the man appeared again sitting atop the same clock as when they'd first walked in. "You kids have spirit. I'll give you that." He tilted his head to the side, surveying them with open curiosity. "And I've read your files, of course. We all have." Another *pop* and he appeared by the far windows, still looking them up and down. "You know, it's a shame that you turned down Stryder's offer of employment, but it isn't too late to recant. Truth be told, I'm sure he'd make the same offer to each of you—"

A cluster of bullets wedged themselves into the wall right where he had been standing, but before they could hit their target the man was already gone. For a second, the three of them just stood there. Breathing rapidly. Wondering where he'd gone.

A second later...they found out.

"Have it your way."

There was a sudden gasp as Julian was lifted clear off his feet and went flying across the room. He didn't hit the wall. He went *through* it, tumbling down the building's top flight of stairs before slamming through the banister on the second story.

Broken shards of wood scattered around him as he made one attempt to get to his feet, then lay still—his eyes closing as a pool of blood soaked through his shirt.

"JULES!"

Devon started racing towards him, when the air around him shimmered and he, too, was lifted off his feet. He vanished with an echoing shout, one hand reaching up behind him and a look of terror frozen permanently on his face.

"DEVON!" Gabriel grasped desperately at the last place his friend had been seen, hoping to feel what was no longer there. He spun around in a frantic circle, heart pounding, waiting for him to reappear, but he never did. Instead, he turned his rage to the teleporter. "I am going to KILL you! You SON OF A BITCH!" His throat hurt from yelling so loud. His hands were trembling with a fury he couldn't control. "SHOW YOURSELF!"

A second later, he froze dead still. The sound of breaking glass filled the air, followed by a muffed crunch. A second after that, a car alarm started screaming from the street down below.

...please, no.

STARING AT THE FUTURE

With a dread that threatened to overpower him, Gabriel made his way to the window. The window that had been somehow smashed open by forces he was unable to see. A rush of cool air swept inside as he leaned over the edge, peering down to the street.

Devon was lying on the hood of a car parked three stories below. The roof was dented in and his limbs were splayed out at odd angles, as if he'd been simply dropped from the sky. His eyes were closed and a crimson pool was spreading around his head like a ghastly halo, filling the cracks and fissures in the metal frame.

Gabriel watched for any sign of life. Watched for even the faintest movement. But there wasn't a sound save for the screaming siren. His friend was terrifyingly still.

He hardly noticed the faint *pop* in the air behind him. Hardly registered the man's presence until he was whispering in his ear. "Still think you made the right decision? Still think Stryder is a man you want as an enemy? Your friends might have begged to disagree..."

Gabriel whipped around with a savage cry, but the man was already gone. Leaving him standing in the middle of an empty room. Blood on the floor. Cold air rushing in from outside.

For a split second, he merely stood there. Trying to gather his senses. Trying to decide which direction to run first. Hoping beyond hope that either friend could be saved. Then a swinging fist came out of nowhere, and struck him right across the temple.

He hit the floor without a sound. His eyes fluttered open and shut, open and shut, before staying closed for good.

Chapter 6

"GABRIEL." A KIND VOICE broke through the endless darkness, beckoning him towards the light. "Gabriel, you need to wake up now."

A faint line creased down the center of his forehead. He felt like his skull had been split open. There was a painful stiffness in his legs that spoke to him being heavily sedated for several hours, and judging by the pricks of pain whenever he flexed his arms he was strapped down on the bed with several hundred IVs.

"Open your eyes, Gabriel."

That voice again. It was gentle, yet firm. The kind of voice that needed to be obeyed. He sincerely tried to do as she asked, opening first one eye, then the other.

Two faces gradually floated into view. One was plump and encouraging. A middle-aged nurse with a radiant smile and glowing brown skin. The other was pale. Tense. Smeared with stains of dried blood. It was a face Gabriel knew almost as well as his own.

"Jules."

It was half-affirmation, half-sigh of relief. The last time he'd seen his future brother-in-law, the man had been thrown through a cinderblock wall and proceeded to fall down the top story of a rickety staircase. Needless to say he wasn't sure he'd be seeing Julian again.

Julian's lips twitched up in a tight smile, one that didn't reach his eyes. There was a tenderness to the way he was cradling his left arm, and judging by the anxious way his eyes kept darting to the nurse he was eager for her to leave and the two of them to be alone.

Of course, that might not have been the only thing troubling him...

"Devon!" Gabriel sat up with a gasp, ignoring the protests of the nurse and the way the room spun the second he was vertical. "Tell me that he's—"

STARING AT THE FUTURE

"You need to lie back down!" the nurse interrupted sternly. As if her words weren't enough, she placed both hands on his shoulders and pressed him firmly onto the bed. He was surprised by how little effort it took her. By how little resistance his own body provided. "You didn't just get a concussion, my friend, you fractured your skull. From now on, your life is going to consist of rest and fluids. Do you understand me?"

Gabriel nodded meekly, but he couldn't take his eyes off Julian. Trying to interpret every micro-expression. Trying to determine whether Devon was alive. "Yes, ma'am."

"Good." She clapped her hands briskly, pleased with his submissive reply. "In that case, I'm going to go and get your doctor. I'm sure he'll be wanting to speak with you."

The two men watched as she strode from the room. Stayed perfectly frozen until the door had shut behind her. Then they sprang to life.

"Is he—"

"Devon's fine." Julian paused suddenly, editing. "I mean—he's not *fine*, but...he's alive." His eyes flickered nervously to the door, worried that at any moment it would open back up again and they would no longer be alone. "Gabriel, we've got to get out of here. If Carter gets wind of the fact that we let ourselves be admitted to a common world hospital... it could start a formal investigation. At the very least, we'll be permanently reassigned to the Yukon."

Gabriel found he needed a second longer than usual to absorb this, probably due to the intense throbbing in his head, but he nodded quickly and swung his legs over the side of the bed. "Right, of course. Let me just..." he paused, staring down at his bare feet as the walls around him danced and swayed, "...where are my clothes?"

"I don't know," Julian said, quickly digging around in a plastic bag. He, too, was oddly dressed—wearing the same pants he'd been that morning, but sporting an oversize sweatshirt that simply read NYC Health. "They didn't have much at the gift shop, so I raided the supply closet instead. Here." He tossed a pair of scrubs Gabriel's way. "These should fit."

Gabriel stared for a minute before slipping the aquamarine shirt over his head. It drowned him. As did the pants. Fortunately, those came with an elastic band. His gaze met Julian's for only a split second before the psychic rolled his eyes and offered a hand up.

"All right, so they don't fit at all. It was the best I could do."

Together, the two men made their way out of the room and down the hall. It was far easier said than done. Not only did Gabriel appear to have no balance whatsoever, but Julian was clearly in worse shape than his stoic face and stolen sweatshirt was letting on.

"Hey, not so hard," he murmured, loosening Gabriel's grip on his shoulder as they darted and tripped down the hall. Luckily, it was the middle of the night, and the place was clearly staffed with the bare minimum. "You'll rip my stitches."

"Sorry." Gabriel pulled back at once, realizing for the first time that his hand was wet with blood. His eyes flickered automatically to the baggy sweater, tightening with sudden concern. "Hey, *truth*: are you okay? Why are you still dressed?"

Julian's eyes flashed momentarily white before he quickly pulled them into a supply closet. They stood there in silence for a moment as a pair of nurses swept past, chatting animatedly about their plans for the end of summer. "I refused treatment," Julian whispered, watching the shadows beneath the door to make sure they had gone. "Got stitched up, then signed out against medical advisement."

Gabriel shot him a look, and he rolled his eyes again.

"I'm fine, all right? I'll see Alicia when we get back to London." He carefully opened the door again, peering out into the empty hall. "At any rate, we can't afford to stay. The hospital is bad enough, but I'm sure it's only a matter of time before the police show up, too."

Gabriel nodded stiffly, following his friend out into the hall. They still had no idea where Devon was being held. Let alone in what state he might be in. All the doctor had told Julian was that both friends he'd been brought in with were alive.

"This is impossible," Julian muttered in frustration. "He's either on a boatload of drugs, or he's sedated. Either way, he's not making any decisions I can follow."

"Then we'll log into the system." Gabriel ducked behind the nurse's station, feeling beneath the desk for a list of passwords. Sure enough, an index card was taped underneath the main console. "As long as he was formally admitted, we should be able to see where he..."

STARING AT THE FUTURE

That's when they heard the singing.

"Oh, crap." Julian's face went pale. "It's worse than I thought."

Gabriel simply froze, listening as a cheerful voice took them through the first lilting verse of "Riders on the Storm". "You have to admit...it's a classic."

"Let's just get the heck out of here."

It didn't take long to find him. Between their friend's soaring vocals and his apparent proclivity to morphine, a small crowd had already assembled in his room.

And with good cause.

To say that Devon was high on painkillers would be understating it. The man was the star of his own little musical.

Considering that he'd been dropped from a three-story apartment, the man didn't look half bad. There was a cast on his leg and a brace on both arms, but with the ocean of drugs pumping through his veins he couldn't feel any of it. Neither could he feel the ghastly array of lacerations splintered across his face and hands, or the heavy bruising that was snaking up his neck.

He was perched upon the headboard of his cot. One hand gripping the remote control as he flipped through television channels at a million miles a minute, while the other pressed periodically upon the button for his IV, trying in vain to get even more morphine.

"Mr. Wardell—" the same nurse who'd chided Gabriel just a few moments before had her hands full yet again, but try as she might it was nearly impossible to look at Devon without smiling. "Mr. Wardell, why don't you try coming down for a moment—"

"His reflexes are off the charts," the doctor murmured, gazing in wonder at his clipboard. "To be honest, as long as he's up and moving I'd love to run some more tests..."

Gabriel and Julian shot each other a quick look but before they could say anything to intervene Devon hopped down off the bed, landing effortlessly on one foot. Despite his awkward cast, he made his way gracefully across the room, tapping the board with a smile. "You think that's off the charts? That's nothing." A flicker of excitement danced in his eyes as he moved a few steps back, preparing for his big moment. "Watch this—"

"Dev!"

"No!"

Both Julian and Gabriel shouted at the same time, forgetting their attempts to be incognito as they hurried to stop their friend from making a mistake he would never be able to take back. The doctor and nurses looked over in surprise but Devon merely straightened up with a beaming smile, thrilled to have an even greater audience for his performance.

"Oh great, guys, you're here!" His words were slurred and untroubled, a testament to the massive amounts of chemicals being pumped through his veins. "I was right about to—"

"—to sit back down before you do something you might regret," Julian interrupted quickly, throwing an arm around his friend's shoulders with a strained smile. "Right, Devon?"

Devon's face clouded with confusion, and he pushed absentmindedly on the button to give himself more drugs. "No. I was not about to do that."

Gabriel bit down upon his lip, and turned quickly to the doctor. "We're going to be checking out a bit earlier than expected, I'm afraid. Are there discharge papers to sign?"

"*Discharge* papers?!" There was a whispered hush through the nurses as the doctor looked at them in astonishment. "Your friend has at least fourteen broken bones, *you*, sir, have what could be a depressed skull fracture, and *you*—" he turned to Julian in dismay, noting the steady spread of blood leaking out from his mangled shoulder, "you won't even let us properly examine you!"

"Yeah, uh..." Julian shoved his hair out of his face, panting with the strain of keeping a hold on Devon, "we're more into homeopathic remedies ourselves..."

"Homeopathic remedies!" The doctor threw up his hands in frustration. "You're going to cure his broken leg with some licorice root and belladonna?"

"Dude," Devon's face grew serious as he turned to Julian for the first time, "we should totally pick up some licorice on the way back to Natasha's."

"Gentlemen," the doctor couldn't sound more strained, "*please* allow us to continue your treatment here. I understand a basic aversion to hospitals, but I can assure you—"

"My aunt's a wiccan," Gabriel explained as he flashed a tight smile. "I'm sure we'll manage." He scribbled something hastily and illegible on the first paper that was shoved under his nose. A second later, Julian held a pen in Devon's hand and forced him to do the same thing. Just a few moments after that, they were back on the grimy streets of New York City. Still dressed in an odd assort-

STARING AT THE FUTURE

ment of gift shop loot and surgical scrubs. Trying their best to make it to the subway before Devon decided once again to break into song.

"This is great, isn't it?" He threw his hands around the others' necks, grinning as he tilted his head back to catch the evening breeze. "Just the three of us. Out in the big city."

Across the street a pair of teenagers started pounding away at each other in a profanity-laced brawl, while on the sidewalk right ahead of them an old woman dumped what looked like a bucket of raw sewage onto the cement.

"That's right, buddy." Julian panted, and shifted Devon out of the line of fire. "We're living the dream."

"I still don't know how you possibly survived," Gabriel murmured, eyes fixed intently on the sidewalk as he helped his friend limp along. "Either one of you. I thought for sure..."

Julian flashed him a quick look, but Devon only smiled. "It would take more than a little push out the window to do away with me," he boasted, pausing only a moment to marvel at the soft texture of Gabriel's hair. "You'll have to redouble your efforts, my friend."

"*My* efforts." This time, even Gabriel had to chuckle. "You think this whole thing has been some elaborate strategy where I try to lure you across the Atlantic to your death?"

"I would be highly offended if it was anything else."

Julian flashed a reluctant grin and steered them over to a bench, lowering Devon down as he fished around in his pocket. A moment later, he came up with a bottle of pills. "How are you doing on pain? They might have loaded you up with the IV, but when that morphine wears off that leg's going to give you hell."

Devon pursed his lips, clapping Julian's damaged shoulder with an affectionate smile. "So, you lifted me something from the hospital pharmacy?"

Julian rolled his eyes and rattled the pills. "Just take *one*. This is the same thing the doctor was going to give you in a few hours. It should do the trick." He glanced down to screw the top back on the lid, and Devon cheerfully popped three pills into his mouth. "In fact, Gabriel, you should probably take one yourself. Your head's got to be killing you."

Gabriel glanced down, but shook his head. "I'm not the one who got thrown through a wall. If one of us is going to stay clear, it's going to be me. Take a pill yourself."

Julian hesitated a moment, then popped one into his mouth. His eyes winced shut for a moment, then he rotated his arm slowly in front of him. "So, what are we going to do?"

"Get some pizza," Devon answered promptly. The others looked down incredulously, and he hastened to explain. "It's *New York City*, right? Home of the world's best pizza?"

Gabriel sighed, raking his bloody hair away from his face. "We need to get him off the streets. Before he starts staging his own Broadway show."

"Julian, I *really* want some pizza," Devon whined. "I think I need some. For my leg."

The psychic helped him up with a wince, looking a bit unsteady on his own feet. "When we get back to the apartment, I'll order in some pizza."

"Do you—"

"I promise."

Finally satisfied, Devon strode briskly across the sidewalk, completely ignoring the fact that he had two recently dislocated arms and a fractured leg. The pain meds put a spring in his step and a smile on his face, until he suddenly stopped, turning to Gabriel with wide eyes. "Gabriel, wait a second."

Both men stopped immediately, thrown off balance by the sudden seriousness in their friend's eyes.

Devon stared at him for a full minute, looking absurdly grave, before a little smile began creeping up the sides of his face. "This girl...do you love her?"

Julian turned away to hide his laughter, while Gabriel clapped Devon on the back with a strained smile and pointed him, once again, in the direction of the apartment.

"Come on. Let's get you inside."

CONSIDERING WHAT THEY were working with, the journey back to Brooklyn was a relatively easy one. They had to stop once or twice for Julian to get his bleeding under control, and Devon was flat-out devastated when the

STARING AT THE FUTURE

others wouldn't let him adopt a stray pigeon. But other than that, they made it back to Natasha's apartment without anyone being the wiser.

"There you go, nice and easy." Gabriel helped Devon up the last of the stairs, guiding him gently down the hall. "Just a few more steps, and then—"

"Well, look who finally decided to come home!"

The apartment fell dead quiet as the three of them froze in place, staring in shock at the teleporter sitting on the couch across the room. His feet were propped up on the gouged coffee table, but when he saw them walk inside he stood up with a gracious smile. A smile that only widened as he looked at each of them in turn.

"Let me guess...depressed skull fracture?" He turned from Gabriel to Julian. "A shattered collarbone and a couple of broken ribs. And *you*?" His eyes came to rest on Devon. "Well, I honestly can't believe you're even alive."

The others stepped automatically in front of Devon, who stood up on his toes so he could still see. No matter which way they chose to approach the situation, things didn't look good. Not only were all three of them thoroughly out of commission from their brief stint at the hospital, but it was clear they were unable to fight this man on their best day. Luck alone had kept them alive the last time, and Gabriel wasn't sure how many more hits they could take.

"They were leaving," he said softly, taking a step forward and angling his body in between, "back to England. If this goes further, you leave them out of it. Deal with me."

"Like—" Julian began, but he needn't have bothered. The teleporter had no intention whatsoever of letting the others walk away. In for a penny, in for a pound.

"Well, that would be a pretty thought indeed, wouldn't it?" He laughed, stretching his arms out in what Gabriel recognized to be his own jacket. "Except that they're not really going back to England. In fact, none of you is ever leaving this room."

"Please," Gabriel urged as the man took a step forward. He wouldn't hesitate to beg. Not when the lives of his friends were on the line. "This is between me and Stryder. Let them go, and I'll come with you willingly. Wherever he wants to meet. His terms, not mine."

And only one coffin will be sent back to England.

"Don't you get what's happening?" The teleporter put his hands on his hips, staring at Gabriel with honest disbelief. "Why you keep getting outmaneuvered? You *care* about people now. They're tethered around you. Like a noose to the neck."

As if to illustrate his point, there was a faint pop and the man disappeared. A second later he flashed back into existence, just long enough to hit Devon over the back of the head and slam Julian's face into the wall.

They fell noiselessly to the floor. Lambs to the slaughter.

Another *pop* and the man appeared back in the far corner, watching with a morbid sort of curiosity as Gabriel knelt beside them, laying a hand on each one.

"You were one of the greats," he muttered, shaking his head with a sullen sort of disappointment, "someone we all aspired to be. Sure, you had your little sister, but the two of you never gave a toss about anything or anybody. It made you invincible." He spat on the floor, taking Gabriel's concern for his fallen comrades personally. "*That* Gabriel Alden would never have found himself in this position. He would have already bagged my head to present to his master on a silver platter."

"Like you intend to do to me?" Gabriel looked up slowly, matching the man stare for vicious stare. "Stryder doesn't have Cromfield's standards, but I can still recognize talent when I see it. You aren't like the other thugs he's sent my way. You see the bigger picture." There was a fleeting pause. "Which is why you *have* to know what will happen if you kill these two men."

He pushed to his feet, keeping the man fixed in his piercing gaze.

"They're agents of the Privy Council. Hand-picked by Carter himself. Kill them, and you'll have the wrath of the entire agency upon you. That is...if you're lucky."

For the first time, a flicker of doubt flashed across the teleporter's face. His eyes darted between Julian and Devon's bodies before returning to Gabriel with a trace of fear.

"That's Devon Wardell," Gabriel said quietly. "He's married to Rae Kerrigan." He paused slightly for effect. "Surely you remember her? The girl who defeated Cromfield? Ability to use any tatù under the sun? Is that really a woman you want to call your enemy?" He took a step closer, pointing now at Julian. "And my little sister? The one who never gave a crap about anything or any-

STARING AT THE FUTURE

body? She's in love with that man. What do you think Angel Cross would do to the man who murdered him?"

The teleporter took a step back as Gabriel slowly shook his head. Almost chidingly. As if the man had let himself fall into a rather obvious trap.

"No. You touch either of them, and your fate is sealed. But accept my offer," he stopped moving, holding his hands in plain sight, "take me to Stryder, and all of this goes away. *You* can still walk away. Nothing that happened today is permanent."

It was quiet for a long time. A very long time. The teleporter stood stiffly by the sofa, staring unblinkingly at the two men. And Gabriel stood calmly in between. Never letting the man out of his sight.

For a split second, he thought it might have worked. For a split second, he thought his friends were in the clear. Then the teleporter started laughing.

It was a wicked sound. Harsh and grating. One that Gabriel knew he would remember for as long as he lived. His eyes narrowed as the man took a step forward, gesturing to the bodies with a careless wave of his hand.

"You truly are as good as they say," he applauded. "I'm serious. For a minute there, you almost had me. But then I realized something very important...*I don't care.*"

The silence exploded as several things happened at once.

Gabriel lifted his hands with a savage cry, at the same time that the teleporter picked up a fallen paperweight and vanished into thin air. A second later that very same weight hit Gabriel across the side of the face, striking him in exactly the same location as the last time the two of them had met. A shocking pain exploded behind his eyes, momentarily blinding him as he fell to the floor. The world around him flickered on and off, darker and darker, fainter and fainter, before his ears pricked up with a sudden metallic click. The unmistakable sound of a gun.

He managed to pry his eyelids open, looking up to see the teleporter pointing the weapon not at his chest but at his head. A faint smile drifted across the man's face, something almost like a goodbye, before he flicked off the safety and slowly squeezed the trigger.

"Now, I know you're a little resistant to these things, but try your best. For me."

The man's fingers tightened, and Gabriel pulled in a sharp breath. His hands twitched, but he was in no condition to use his ink. He was in no condition to do anything other than lie there, waiting for the sharp sting of the bullet.

But it was a bullet that would never come.

A flash of neon blue shot through the air, knocking the man back. Another flash and the gun flew out of his hand, dropping out the open window. There was a soft crunch of shoes upon glass, and Gabriel lifted his head to see a pair of high-heeled combat boots. Two pairs, in fact. Each one planted on either side.

"It's going to take a lot more than a gun to get through his thick skull..."

Chapter 7

YOU KNOW THAT MOMENT in a movie where it seems all hope is gone, but then a hero shows up at the last second and suddenly you can breathe again? Growing up in a cave, Gabriel had never been allowed to watch those movies. But over the years, he'd been in enough life or death situations to be very familiar with the real thing.

"Ladies," he let his head drop back to the floor with an exhausted sigh, "always a pleasure to see you."

Rae Kerrigan took a step forward, her eyes dancing with ice blue flames as the teleporter shrank back before her.

Molly Skye was right by her side, a shower of electric sparks raining down from her hands as she glanced around what remained of the ramshackle apartment. "And here I predicted whatever place they were staying at would be a dump." Her tiny nose shriveled up with distaste as a piece of molded plaster fell from the wall. "I clearly overestimated things..."

Rae was far less distractible. And far more ticked off. Probably something that had to do with the fact that her husband was lying on the floor. Bleeding profusely. "For Pete's sake, Alden," she murmured. "How many times am I going to burst in on you with a gun pointed at your head? A *gun* pointed at his head," she echoed to Molly, casting an accusatory glance over her shoulder. "Still think we should have stopped at Starbucks?"

Molly flushed guiltily, sinking to the floor to take Julian's pulse. The second she located it she did the same with Devon, keeping her eyes locked on the teleporter the whole time. "They're alive." Gone was the playful edge to her voice. It was replaced with something different. Something scary. "For now."

Rae tilted her head to the side, staring at the teleporter with a look that sent chills running up and down Gabriel's arms. "Well, that's the first, and I suspect the last, bit of luck you're going to have today. If my husband was already dead, this would have been a different conversation."

Not a conversation so much as a ritualistic slaughter.

The teleporter gulped and took another step backwards, visibly shaken. His muscles tensed, then relaxed, then tensed up again as the remainder of Molly's deadly voltage slowly made its way through his system. One eye was twitching, and his breath came in short bursts.

Take him down, Gabriel tried to speak, but he was too weak. *Take him down before he recovers from the shock. Take him down before he kills you.*

A legitimate threat, but he needn't have worried. The girls clearly had things well under control.

Not long after the battle at the sugar factory, both Rae and Molly had been officially paired up as partners. The decision made a lot of sense. Not only had the girls already been working together for years, but you were unlikely to find a more potent and terrifying combination of powers anywhere else in the agency. It didn't take long for them to establish themselves a reputation that went above and beyond the acclaim that defeating Cromfield had already brought them. They broke all the records. Shot the agency curb to hell. Took down enough high priority targets that the Council was actually considering renaming a wing of the building in their honor. The inked community adored them. They were revered beyond measure.

In fact, one of the only people who wasn't thrilled with their success at the agency was Rae's own husband. No, he and Julian weren't thrilled. They were competitive.

It had become something of an office joke. A constant source of entertainment as the cases were assigned, and the people scurrying about in the tunnels below Guilder made their weekly bets. Gambling on the clash of the gods.

Back when they were just teenagers, the men had established themselves as the agency hotshots. The impossible standard against which all other agents were measured. They had scaled the ladder faster than anyone who had come before, and when a particularly dangerous case came about they were the ones who were automatically expected to bring it home.

Until now.

Now, the playing field was split. Now, those impossible cases were evenly divided. And while a part of them might be secretly elated for their friends, each team would love nothing more than to publicly tear the other down. It was a game they had all won and lost many times.

Carter loved it. And used it constantly to his own advantage. Preying on their egos and insecurities. Sending both teams out at once, so that he and Beth could end up watching Aria back in London. If Rae and Devon hadn't gotten wise to his scheme and formally insisted that only one of them be sent out of the country at a time, there's no telling how long he might have kept them away—fighting drug lords in Peru while he played hopscotch with their daughter.

Parental restrictions aside, the competition raged on. Fierce as ever. And, needless to say, this was a day that would live in infamy for the men...

"So...what's your little trick?" Rae glanced at the man's bare arm with the hint of a frown. "I don't recognize the ink."

Nor had she ever seen the three strongest men in her life laid out by what looked like a single opponent. The banter was a front. She and Molly were watching the man very carefully.

"He's a teleporter," Gabriel panted, trying to pull himself up to a sitting position and failing spectacularly. "Working Stryder's for...I mean...my friend kidnapped his apartment..." No, that wasn't right either. He brought a hand to his temple as the girls shot him an incredulous look. "Sorry...he broke my head."

Molly and Rae shared a glance as Gabriel fell silent, then stepped forward at the same time. Half to gauge the man's opposition. Half to shield their friends from view.

"Teleportation, huh?" Despite her caution, Rae's face lit with an almost childlike excitement. "I've been dying to get my hands on that one."

"You want it, girly?" The man stepped back, spreading his arms as his hands curled into gnarled fists. "Come and get it."

There was a faint *pop*, and Gabriel's breath caught in his chest. This could *not* be happening again. He could not have just seen the bravest men he knew fall victim to this psychopath, only to have to watch it happen to the women as well.

But Rae and Molly had no intention of playing the victim. Not today, not ever.

The second the man disappeared, Molly raised her hands with a little smile. Her fiery hair crackled with electricity as it haloed in a cloud around her, shimmering in the moonlight as if it was propelled by its own wind. She didn't stop to aim, didn't stop to think. Instead, she spread her arms wide and fired off a round of lightning unlike anything Gabriel had ever seen.

His eyes fluttered open and shut as he gazed in wonder above him. She hadn't aimed for the place the man had been standing. Instead, she'd created an electric dome. A spiderweb of lightning that arched over the ceiling of the warehouse. Flickering like a little cage.

A second later, that cage got its first prisoner.

There was a burst of sparks, followed by a hoarse scream. The dome flickered for a moment before the teleporter fell from the ceiling, reappearing as he hit the floor.

Rae didn't waste a moment.

The second the man was back in view, she curved her hand through the air like a potter working their clay. A metal chair appeared out of nowhere, falling to the floor with a deafening clatter. What looked like a thin, steel rope appeared by its side, curling up in the air like a live snake, just waiting to ensnare its victim.

The fact that Rae could now use all her tatùs at once meant that, in theory, she never had to move a muscle. She could simply stand there, and use the magic flowing through her veins to get the job done.

But Rae Kerrigan had never been one for standing still. She was known to get her hands dirty. Especially when the fate of her friends hung in the balance.

Instead of using a basic levitation charm she raced forward, blurring through the air before jumping up for a flying tackle. She caught the teleporter just as he was pushing back off the floor, flipping her body in a graceful arch that simultaneously shoved him into the chair.

"Kerrigan," Molly chided, sounding bored, "this is no time for gymnastics."

Rae flashed her a grin, one arm circled around the man's throat. "Sorry. Got a little bit carried away."

"Carried away?" the teleporter hissed through his teeth.

She silenced him with a single punch.

From there, the ropes took over—wrapping around his legs, arms, and chest like they had a mind of their own—before shooting through the air into Molly's waiting hand.

STARING AT THE FUTURE

"How does that feel?" Rae asked routinely, smoothing down her shirt like the two of them were simply discussing what dress to wear to the next family gathering.

Molly gave the rope an experimental tug and a shockwave of electricity shot through it, circling and twisting around before finding the metal chair. The man let out a quick shout, then suddenly fell silent—panting—as he waited for the next burst.

"Feels good."

Rae nodded calmly, glancing back at the teleporter. "And how does that feel to you?"

"You BIT—"

Another shock and the man fell silent, twitching and writhing in pain. Molly blinked back at him, winding the rope around her wrist like a bracelet. "I'm sorry, what was that?"

For the second time, Gabriel's head fell back against the floor with a sigh of relief. Rae whirled around immediately, leaving the teleporter to Molly as she knelt beside him.

"It's okay. You're okay." She picked up his head and lay it in her lap, smoothing back his hair so she could get a better look at the gash by his temple. There was a sympathetic wince then she stroked a finger gently over it, healing as she went. "So, you broke your head, huh?"

"*I* didn't do it." He cast her a sullen look. "*He* did."

"Sure." She pursed her lips and carried on with a little smile, gripping him comfortingly as her hands worked their healing magic. "You know, a lot of us would say there's been something wrong with your head for years. I'm not sure your problems all started today—"

"You're *so* funny." He pushed to a tentative sitting position; already his head was beginning to clear. "That's why I stayed away so long. To avoid that searing wit."

She snorted and held up her hand. "How many fingers?"

"Twelve. That's good, right?"

She laughed again, and the two of them exchanged a fleeting look. One that conveyed all those complex emotions they were unable to say. The smiles turned tender, and for a split second he reached out and squeezed her hand. A silent thank-you. Worth more than words.

"Well, then," she briskly shook back her hair, pushing to her feet, "if you'll excuse me, I have a husband to revive. Then murder."

Gabriel cast a sympathetic look over his shoulder to where Devon and Julian were both still passed out on the floor. There was no longer any overt bleeding, but it was clear that the two were in bad shape. Even worse than when they'd left the hospital.

"Honey?" Rae gently rolled Devon onto his back, brushing back his dark hair as she gazed down at his battered body, her eyes lingering on the cast and the two braces covering his arms. "You need to wake up."

Nothing. He was out cold.

"Sweetie," she whispered, lowering her lips to his ear, "Aria got into your shaving cream again..."

A jolt shot through his body and his eyes snapped open, staring around in a daze before finally settling on the lovely face of his wife. A wife who was just as angry as she was beautiful.

"There you are." She pressed a tender kiss to his forehead, then leaned back and slapped him across the face. "Now do you want to tell me what the freakin' A is going on?"

FIVE MINUTES LATER, everyone was awake (for the most part), standing (for the most part), and were attempting to explain what had happened over the last few days.

Not that the explanation was going over particularly well...

"Oh, good," Rae's enthused, eyes narrowed as they flickered to the plastic bands circling her husband's wrists, "hospital ID tags."

Devon held up his hands. "Honey, it's not as bad as it seems—"

"You're not wearing any pants."

He glanced down. Along with Gabriel and Julian. How had they possibly missed that? "Yeah...but my jacket's really long."

Rae closed her eyes, pressing her fingers to her temples. "And you're high."

Devon straightened up at once, trying to look as normal and put together as possible. It was a plan that was only slightly ruined by the fact that he couldn't stop playing with his zipper.

STARING AT THE FUTURE

Sensing the need for an assist Julian leaned forward, gently clutching the parts of his shoulder that Rae had been unable to fully heal. "Rae, in his defense, they're all prescription. Checked the bottle myself—"

"And *you*!" She whirled around, almost angrier than she'd been with the other two. "*You* are supposed to be the grounded one! The one I can trust to keep things like this from happening, and to *call me* if these two idiots get in over their heads!"

He bowed his head, accepting the censure without a word. But Rae wasn't finished. She and Molly had raced to Brooklyn, expecting to help the rest of the gang with whatever foolhardy scheme they'd concocted. They certainly hadn't expected to find them half-dead on the floor.

"How would you like it if I told Angel about this?!"

Gabriel hadn't really expected that threat to go over well, but Julian took it even worse than Gabriel could have imagined. Jules' entire face tightened, and he looked at Rae with the mix of a warning and a plea. Fortunately, she was too distracted to maintain the threat for long.

"Hey!" Molly called. "As much as I love zapping this guy every thirty seconds, do you think we could move this part of things along?"

"This is my fault." Gabriel pushed to his feet, easing in between Devon and Rae, putting his hands on her shoulders. "Jules and Devon came here for me. Everything that's happened since then...I've been directly responsible. They've only tried to help."

"So, what are you saying?" Her mouth thinned into a hard line as she cocked her head back towards the teleporter. "Should I conjure up another chair?"

Gabriel's gaze flickered to the prisoner before returning to hers with a faint grin. "Rae, if you really want to tie me up, I can think of better ways for us to pass the time..."

She stared at him for a split second, then shocked him in between the ribs. "Unbelievable. Even when you're supposed to be apologizing."

He straightened up with a painful gasp as Devon roughly shoved him aside.

"Sweetheart, I'm sorry we didn't call. *Really*, I am. And if you want to blame this entire thing on Gabriel—I think that's a fantastic idea. But, in the meantime, I really need to interrogate the prisoner." He took her hand with a coaxing smile. "So maybe we could shelve this discussion for later, and you could conjure me some pants...?"

Rae hesitated for a moment, staring into those twinkling eyes.

Then she shocked him as well.

FIVE MINUTES LATER, they had yet to make much headway.

"—and I promise we'll get back to that, as I wasn't aware there was a 'transcontinental rule.' But you still haven't answered my question. Who has our daughter?"

Rae and Devon were squaring off in the center of the room. One looking armed and dangerous in her official PC mission gear. The other looking slightly less so in the neon-orange sweatpants Rae had finally deigned to conjure.

"Our daughter is *fine*," Rae answered sarcastically. "I didn't just leave her to fend for herself, you know. I dropped her off with my mom."

There was a split-second pause, during which everyone in the room flinched.

"...*your* mom?"

Even Rae had the sense to look slightly guilty. "Yeah. Why?"

Devon cocked his head to the side, somehow managing to look intimidating despite the strange attire his wife had forced him to wear. "Oh, I don't know, maybe because it's *my parents' turn*?!" She opened her mouth to reply, but he beat her to the punch. "Babe, *I* couldn't care less about the schedule, but they're going to be pissed! You know they are!"

"I'm sorry." Rae put her hands on her hips, looking not sorry at all. "I'm sorry that I didn't have time to drive all the way to Esher, before Molly and I had to hop on a plane to come and save your ass! It was bad enough convincing our handler to give us twelve hours on the way to Calgary so we could detour to freaking Brooklyn!"

A good point, but with a fatal flaw. One her husband zeroed in on with shocking speed.

"*Calgary?*" He raised his eyebrows dangerously. "And why are you flying to Canada, dear? I thought you were taking time off this month to stay home with Aria."

STARING AT THE FUTURE

Rae tilted her head to the side with a sweet smile. "Well, someone has to work to pay your exorbitant hospital bills."

A ringing silence descended upon the room. A silence that no one seemed willing to break. Eventually, it was the teleporter himself who cleared his throat with an apologetic cough.

"Not to break this up...but can we get back to me, please?"

"Absolutely." Gabriel strode forward without another word, punching the man in the face with enough force to instantly break his jaw. "Where's Natasha?" Before he could answer, there was another punch. This one was even harder than the first. "Don't make me ask twice."

The man turned with a gasp and spat a mouthful of blood onto the floor as a strong hand wrapped around Gabriel's arm pulling him back a step.

"He can't tell us anything if you break his jaw," Julian reminded quietly.

"I'll ask yes or no questions," Gabriel replied through gritted teeth. "He can point to the place on a damn map."

Julian carefully looked him over, those dark eyes seeing everything whether they were in the future or the past. "Or you can step outside and let Devon and me handle this."

"*Step outside*?!" Gabriel wrenched his arm free in surprise. "Are you kidding?"

"You're too deep into this," Julian interrupted softly, his voice as steady as it was strangely persuasive. "It's too personal. This is why Dev and I are here. Let us help you."

"Help me interrogate him, then—"

"Gabriel, we're not going to get anywhere if I sit back and let you beat him to death."

No, but it would be deeply satisfying.

Gabriel froze perfectly still for a moment, staring over Julian's shoulder with a look of the deepest loathing, then he turned abruptly on his heel. "You have ten minutes."

Without another word he left the apartment, flying down the crumbling stairwell, not stopping until he came out on the open street. The cold night air bit into his cheeks, and he pulled in deep breaths to steady himself.

Natasha was out there somewhere. Maybe closer than he thought. Just ten more minutes, and this guy was going to give up the location. Then Gabriel could finally take her home.

He should have guessed what would happen next. Should have known that she wasn't going to let him go off by himself. Not when he was so upset.

"So, did Devon make you guys stop for 'New York pizza' yet?"

He smiled to himself and held out his arm, head still tilted back to the stars. "He sincerely tried. Then he got distracted trying to catch a bird."

Rae slipped under his arm with a giggle. "That's my man. You guys know what he's like on painkillers. I'm surprised you didn't just make him breathe through it."

"Why?" Gabriel shot her a sideways smile. "And give you two nothing to fight about?" The smile was there, but his voice lacked the mischief it used to. Even his eyes were having trouble keeping up with the lackluster grin.

Rae seemed to think so, too. "What's the matter?" She slipped her arm around his waist and gave him a gentle squeeze. "You usually love it when Devon and I argue. The last time, you actually made popcorn and pulled a chair onto the lawn."

He opened his mouth to answer, then closed it again with a shrug. He was having trouble caring too deeply about anything. Save for one beautiful, lost face.

Rae studied him for a moment, then moved them carefully past it. The two of them knew each other too well by now to pry. If there was something there, it would come out in time. "So, we've got another mini-crime syndicate on our hands?"

Gabriel's shoulders fell with a sigh. "They've metastasized to Brooklyn—the remainder of Cromfield's employees." He glanced down again at Rae before a belated shudder ran through his tired body. "Thanks for coming, really. I don't know what would have...anyway, thanks."

"Don't mention it." She flashed him a bright smile, her eyes lit with a curiosity she was trying very hard to contain. "So, Julian tells me this girl you're looking for specializes in memory retrieval. She's leading you on some sort of spirit quest?"

Gabriel's chest tightened, but he forced himself to be calm. "Yeah, something like that."

STARING AT THE FUTURE

She hesitated, then lifted her eyes again. "She's helping you find your dad?"

He flashed her a look, but stayed silent. Of all the people in his life, she alone knew the constant struggle he had with his father. Of his inability to let the man go.

A comfortable silent settled between them before he finally broke it with a soft sigh.

"Your father couldn't give you up to Cromfield," he said quietly. "He made a promise, but he couldn't go through with it. Mine could." His chest tightened again, and it was suddenly a challenge just to keep breathing. "I need to understand how he could do that. How he could just...give me away. Like it was nothing."

His voice was almost a whisper by the end. A rare bit of vulnerability shone through the cracks, and Rae squeezed her arm around him once more.

"And that's what this girl is helping you to find out?"

He paused for a moment, then lifted his eyes to the clear night sky. "...she's helping me find a lot of things."

Rae stared up at him for a second more, but said not a word. A knowing little smile danced behind her eyes, but he would never see it. Not until Natasha was back and the whole mess was over with. Not until he was ready.

And on that note...

"Hey, guys?" They glanced up to see Devon looking down from the window. "The guy won't break."

Gabriel glanced down at his watch. "Ten minutes. My turn."

They were back inside the next moment, moving purposefully into the apartment where the interrogation had reached an obvious pause. Although the teleporter was clearly worse for the wear, the man wasn't talking. And they were running out of time.

"All right." Gabriel didn't break stride as he made his way inside, ripping off a piece of the metal door frame and holding it like a crowbar. "Let's see if you can be persuaded."

"Hey, hey, hey!" Devon stopped him, putting a light hand on his chest. "Jules is right: it's not going to help anyone if you kill him."

Gabriel's eyes narrowed with a chilling smile. "You underestimate how much pain a person can go through and still be alive."

"I'm serious," he urged, lowering his voice, "pain isn't working. Trust me, we haven't exactly been going easy on the guy. We need to figure out whatever's motivating him. Maybe then—"

"Oh, please." Molly rolled her eyes with a look of great impatience. "Just let me do it."

The men looked over in surprise as she abandoned her perch on the kitchen counter and swept confidently toward the prisoner. Ignoring the puddles of blood gathered around him, she tossed back her hair and whispered something into the guy's ear.

Gabriel could honestly say it was one of the strangest things he'd ever seen.

The man went pure white. Not some shade of it. White. His eyes flashed up for the briefest of moments, staring at Molly like she was a nightmare come to life. Then he lifted his finger and pointed to an address on the city map. One on the other side of town.

"There," she said, straightening briskly, and went back to her friends, "that wasn't so hard."

The others stared in open fascination as the unbreakable teleporter slumped down in his chair and quietly began to cry.

"What did you say to him?" Devon asked in amazement, looking like a part of him almost didn't want to know.

Molly just smirked. "The same thing I say to Benjamin when he won't eat his vegetables." She and Rae shared a quick look, then she tapped her watch. "We're running late."

Rae nodded quickly, and turned back to the man. "I wish we could stay and help you guys finish this, but we're on the clock with this other thing in Canada. And when I say we got permission to come here first...I might have been stretching that a bit."

Devon laughed and gathered her up for a huge hug. "Be safe, love. I don't like it when I'm not there to watch your back."

She raised her eyebrows, giggling when he lifted her clear off the floor. "Hasn't this little experience taught you that it's *me* who watches *your* back? Besides, if anything should happen, I've got this little psycho to keep me company."

Molly flashed a bright smile, then jumped up to kiss Julian on the cheek.

STARING AT THE FUTURE 83

"This should only be a few more days, then I'll meet you back in London," Devon murmured, unwilling to let her go. "I miss you."

She pulled back with a sigh, then kissed him softly on the lips. "I miss you, too. Be careful." She glanced around the room. "All of you. Or *else*."

The men chuckled, and waved goodbye as the women gathered their things and swept out the door.

Molly was already halfway to the stairs, when Rae paused in the doorway and turned back around. She and Gabriel locked eyes from across the room. For a moment, all they did was stare.

Then her lips curved up in a twinkling smile. "Go get your girl."

Chapter 8

THE TELEPORTER WAS placed in a crate, which was loaded onto a shipping container headed for London being sent by air. According to the information slip taped across the front, the crate was to be hand-delivered to a man named Andrew Carter. A belated birthday gift.

There were at least five tatù-inhibitors in the wood itself, as well as three separate devices strapped to the man's person. Between that and the single bottle of water and peanut butter sandwich that had been thrown inside, the reluctant traveler hopefully wouldn't have any delays.

It was a thought that brought an actual smile to Gabriel's lips as he and his two friends bounced and jostled about on the midnight subway heading to the Upper East Side.

A brewing storm around Heathrow... A little spill on the runway...

"What are you so happy about?" Devon demanded, shooting him a hard look from the opposite side of the train. It was deserted, save for one homeless man who was snoring hard in his sleep, and they could talk with relative privacy. "Still imagining all the different ways that man could die?"

Okay, we've got to stop spending so much time together.

Gabriel simply shrugged, unable to fully hide his murderous grin. "Still sulking that your wife and her best friend had to swoop in and save you at the last second?"

He'd obviously touched a nerve. Devon's head fell back against the seat as his hands flew up in exasperation. He'd healed miraculously fast, probably partially courtesy of his tatù. "A midnight rescue? Kicking down the door to find us unconscious at gunpoint in Brooklyn?" His eyes snapped shut with a look of profound despair. "They're never going to let us live it down..."

A few seats over Julian was gently massaging his shoulder, propping his feet up on the adjacent chair as he eyes stared vacantly out the window. "Sometimes,

STARING AT THE FUTURE

85

I just don't get Molly. Last time I saw her, she was researching how to get waffle batter out of Prada. But back there..."

"That's really what you're doing?" Gabriel asked sarcastically. "Trying to unravel the unfathomable mind of Molly Skye? We may need to loop the city a few more times."

"Then there was that whole thing with the pants..." Devon was still muttering to himself, tuning out the others completely. "And in front of the *prisoner*, no less! How many times have I told her not to undermine me in the middle of an interrogation?"

"*Marriage*." Julian shook his head sagely. "They say the first few years are the hardest."

"Yeah?" Devon shot him a wicked smile. "You ready to find out?"

Gabriel glanced over curiously as Julian abruptly turned pale. Fortunately, the psychic was spared from answering when the door to the train opened and a trio of girls climbed inside.

They had clearly just come from a party. Dressed to the nines and reeking of booze, they hardly made it inside teetering precariously on their tall heels. A burst of giggles erupted out of them as they swayed back and forth, holding each other steady. The kind of giggles that made Gabriel deeply grateful that Angel preferred things like semi-automatic weapons to keg stands and nail polish when they were growing up. His patience was already strained, and for a moment he was almost tempted to get out and walk the rest of the way, but the girlish laughter came to an abrupt stop when they looked up and saw who else was on the train.

It was replaced by a flurry of whispers instead.

"Holy smokes! Do you *see* that guy?!"

"I can't decide who's prettier. The one with the light hair, or the one with the dark."

"You girls are crazy; it's definitely the one with the dimples! He's not even smiling, but you can totally tell he has dimples!"

"Do you think they go to NYU?"

"You should ask! But don't ask that one—I have dibs!"

"You know, I'm thinking of applying there myself..."

Devon, who could hear a lot more than the other two, grimaced painfully and angled himself the other way. Julian and Gabriel glanced wistfully at the list of stations. But just wishing time would go faster wasn't going to make it so. That intoxicated pack mentality had taken hold, and nothing in the world was going to get in the women's way.

"Um, excuse me..." A fake blonde with little smudges of mascara clustered around her eyes, leaned flirtatiously across the aisle towards Devon. "Do you know what time it is?"

*All that build-up, and **that's** the line she chose?* Gabriel rolled his eyes while Julian started fake-texting, but the girl clearly thought herself incredibly brave to have spoken, and Devon was too polite not to reply.

"I think it's a little after twelve."

Maybe he should have kept silent after all. The second they heard his accent the girls swooned all over again, instinctively convinced the others must have the same thing.

"Ooooooh my gosh, wait a second!" The girl abandoned her friends entirely, and half-stumbled his way. "Are you guys British?"

Either by design or simply by accident, the train jerked and she went tumbling off her heels with a drunken shriek. Devon pushed to his feet immediately and caught her, flushing all the while, much to the mischievous delight of his friends.

"Uh...yeah." He gently removed her hands from where they'd anchored behind his neck, and lowered her down into the nearest chair. "We're from England."

There was another squeal, followed by another burst of bravery as another of the girls detached herself from the group and sat down in the chair next to Julian.

"I totally knew it! Just by looking at you!"

Since his 'I'm-busy-with-my-phone' excuse clearly wasn't working, Julian slipped it back into his pocket with a strained smile. "Yeah, we're just visiting." With a burst of genius, he gestured across the aisle to Devon. "His wife lives in the city. Along with my girlfriend."

The flirtatious smile slid right off the girl's face, landing in a puddle on the floor. A twin look of disappointment darkened the girl still sitting by Devon. But the third of the women, the one who had yet to make a move, looked like she'd just won the jackpot.

STARING AT THE FUTURE

"What about you?" She cocked her head seductively in Gabriel's direction, pupils dilating hungrily as she looked him up and down. "You single?"

Devon and Julian spoke at the same time, eager to help things along. "Oh, yeah, he's totally single."

"Looking for company, in fact."

"He's way too shy to ever say it himself."

"You kind of have to make the first move, if you know what I mean."

Gabriel's eyes narrowed as he gave each of his friends a look that promised certain death, but the girl needed no more invitation than that.

With a little grin, she slid off her chair and sauntered down the aisle, planting her tall heels right in front of his chair. "Is that true?" Her voice lowered to a seductive purr as she tossed back her long hair to give him a better view of her chest. "You looking for a girl to make the first move?"

Whatever little remained of Gabriel's sense of humor vanished on the spot. His green eyes went abruptly cold, and although his lips twitched up in an obligatory smile there was something about his expression that made the girl take a sudden step back. "I'm looking for a girl who was recently kidnapped," he replied quietly, staring intently into her wide eyes. "We just put the guy who did it in a container back to London, and while we're waiting for confirmation as to whether or not he asphyxiated on the way we're going to burn down your precious little Greenwich Village trying to get this girl back."

The girl's eyes widened as she stumbled back another step. On the other side of the aisle, both Julian and Devon had frozen perfectly still. The entire train went dead quiet, save for the rhythmic pulse of the tracks, and for a second not a single person on board was sure what exactly was going to happen next.

Then the sound of hacking laughter shattered the silence.

"A container? Like a shipping container!" The young people whirled around in surprise as the homeless man who'd been sleeping on the other side of the compartment woke up and shifted onto his side, coughing and chuckling all the while. "That's the best thing I've heard all day."

Gabriel flashed his first genuine smile, deciding abruptly that he'd prefer the man's company to anyone else's. Then, as if on cue, the train slowed to a stop and the door slid open. "Well, this is us." He hopped onto the platform without a second thought, flashing a cheerful smile of farewell at the shell-shocked girls. "Have a better night."

Devon and Julian flashed each other a strained look, then hurried out after him. A second later they were all jogging up the stairs, purposely avoiding looking at the three slack-jawed statues they'd left back on the train.

"Really?" Devon demanded as they swept out into the open air. "Whether or not he asphyxiates? You had to say it?"

"That's right, man." Gabriel clapped him on the shoulder, and headed up the street with the hint of a smile. "I had to say it."

JUST BASED UPON HIS rather limited dealings with Stryder, Gabriel instinctively knew that getting Natasha out of the safe-house was going to be harder than it seemed. The man might have lacked Cromfield's raw power, but that had forced him to get crafty. And so far, that devious craftiness had proven highly effective. Staring up at the industrial loft where he was said to be keeping her, Gabriel wondered ominously at what might be waiting on the other side.

"Jules, can you see anything?" he asked quickly and quietly, not wanting to be heard.

The psychic's eyes glowed ever so briefly in the dark night before clearing back with an expression of pleasant surprise. "Yeah, I can. Stryder's not there."

How was that possible? A man like Stryder didn't make mistakes.

Gabriel shifted uneasily and glanced at Devon, who seemed to be going through the same thought process as him. His bright eyes flickered up to the third-story window for a moment before turning back to Gabriel with a restless sort of anticipation.

"Maybe he thought the teleporter finished us off," he said softly. "Freakin' A, he almost did. If it wasn't for Rae and Molly, none of us would have come out of that fight."

Gabriel followed his gaze back to the window, nodding slowly. No, after meeting the teleporter he wouldn't have bet on any of them making it out alive. Maybe Stryder didn't either. "How many are there?" He turned back to Julian, holding out a hand to steady him as he slipped away into the future. "What do you see if we decide to attack?"

Julian tranced out for a few moments, swaying slightly in the breeze, then blinking back to the present with a small smile. Thus far, his extraordinary gift had been next to no help on this journey. It felt good to be useful again. "There are three of them. Super speed, ice, and a shifter. Can't see what the shifter actually turns into, only that he decides to shift." He caught Gabriel's eye and preempted the question before he could even ask. "I didn't see Natasha. But there's a room in back that they seem to be guarding. No guns. They're used to fighting with their ink."

A flicker of a smile ghosted up Gabriel's face as his eyes returned to the window. It was the only place in the whole building that had a faint glow, and he was suddenly, overwhelmingly convinced that Natasha was behind it. "So, she's here. She's alive."

Devon was bouncing from foot to foot, stretching out his arms and limbering up. His eyes danced with that same anticipatory mischief that had made the PC recruit him straight out of school. "And no one's going to pop up out of thin air? Pull us into some parallel dimension and drop us off the building?" The other two shot him a look, and he was quick to clarify. "Or anything along those lines, doesn't have to be so specific…"

Julian grinned and shook his head. "There's only three. Ice, shifter, and speed." As he spoke he pointed to each of them, assigning the targets as he went along. "No surprises."

"Then let's do it." Devon stopped bouncing and stared up at the window with a singular sort of determination. "You've a girl to save, I've an ego to resuscitate, and you have a—" He caught himself suddenly, throwing Julian a panicked look. "A girlfriend to get back to."

An uncharacteristically dark look came over Julian's face, but Gabriel was too caught up to really notice it. He couldn't take his eyes off the window. He couldn't stop his body moving forward.

"Let's go."

IT TOOK NO TIME TO break into the building. Then barely any time to climb the stairs. And it didn't take long once they were inside to kick down the door and burst inside with that signature PC flair that they'd been sorely missing these last few days.

Julian was right. There were only three men inside. Three men who leapt to their feet the second the door was kicked down, then stared with open bewilderment as they raced inside.

"Evening, gentlemen." Gabriel stepped forward with a smile. "Good to see you again."

All three had been at the market, threatening him with human hostages the morning Natasha was taken. All three had scattered like birds when Gabriel turned the cameras.

It was a rather embarrassing turn of events. One that the men seemed to remember as well.

The tallest of the three stepped forward with a sneer designed to overcompensate. "So...Cromfield's little orphan makes a comeback." His lips curled back to show every one of his rotten teeth. "Tell me, did that boy make it off the street alive? Or did Doug empty his pistol into the kid's ribcage?"

Julian lifted his eyebrows slowly. "Oh, you made some lovely new friends here in Brooklyn."

"What do you expect?" Devon scoffed under his breath. "They're American."

Julian glanced at him sharply. "Your wife's American."

"She was born British. Then renounced the American part."

"That's right, you wouldn't know what happened to the boy." Gabriel kept his eyes on the man, smiling sweetly all the while. "You *ran*."

The sneer was gone. Replaced with an open scowl. "A mistake we aim to remedy right now..."

That was the only bit of warning they got. Like looking in a mirror, three men separately paired off. Each taking a single opponent. Each blurring into action as their ink took hold.

Julian's eyes flashed white as a muscular man on the left lifted his hands and sent a wave of serrated ice flying straight at his head. If it weren't for his ink, it would have impaled him on the spot. As it stood, he back-flipped easily out of the way, taking the opportunity to send a knife of his own flying back through the air, lodging neatly in the man's ribs.

On the other side of the loft, Devon was clearly enjoying what he would refer to as a 'fair fight.' Not that there was anything fair about it. As fast as the fox was, the man he was fighting bore the mark of the cheetah, almost three times

STARING AT THE FUTURE

91

his speed. It was a match that would've sent almost anyone else running for the hills, but Devon Wardell hadn't become a hallowed name for nothing. He'd cut his teeth on worse ink than that when he was sixteen.

The others heard him laughing as he and the man collided in the middle of the room. Felt the shuddering impacts through the floor as the two opponents quickly blurred out of a speed impossible to be seen by human eyes.

Gabriel glanced once to the left and right, then returned his gaze to the man with a little smile. The fight was going to be even easier than he had thought. Over before it had even begun.

And then I'll see Natasha...

Except when he turned back to center, he found he was no longer looking at a man. The man had melted away entirely. Leaving an angry lion in his place.

What the—

The thing let out a deafening roar, and Gabriel fell back in spite of himself—every boyhood fear he'd ever had rising to the surface. For a second, he simply stood there. Stunned. Then the thing leapt towards him, and he somersaulted over the floor.

"A LION, Jules!" he panted, straightening up where the beast had stood just a moment before. "You couldn't have seen that he turned into a freakin' *LION?*"

Across the room, Julian poked his head out from behind a bookcase. His dark hair was streaked with a thick coating of ice, aging him about fifty years. "A lion, really? That's so—"

"NOT cool, Julian!" Gabriel shouted angrily, ripping a sheet of metal off the wall and quickly fashioning it into a makeshift shield. "Do NOT say that it's cool!"

For whatever reason, the creature wasn't reacting to his hold on its blood. Not that he was really surprised. Animals were always a bit harder than people. Mostly because they never held still long enough for him to get a good—

"Holy crap!"

The creature leapt again, and this time there was no getting away. Instead, Gabriel ducked beneath the shield, pushing the lion up and over his head, barely avoiding the massive claws that swiped at the side of his face.

Not quite avoiding them after all.

A sudden rush of blood warmed the side of Gabriel's cheek, and he lifted his fingers to feel five huge claw marks running down the side of his face. His head spun for a moment but he kept low to the ground, countering the creature's every move with the shield held high.

I have been attacked...by a lion. Check that off my bucket list. A second later, another thought occurred to him. One that couldn't help but make him smile. *Angel's going to be so jealous...*

The lion roared again, but this time Gabriel didn't wait for the beast to attack. This time, he threw caution to the wind and charged the creature head-on.

"Gabriel, *don't!*"

He heard Devon's distant cry but kept his eyes on the target, never changing course.

There came a point in a man's life where the rules of logic failed him, and there was no choice but to act on pure instinct. Gabriel was fighting a lion. Why not charge?

His golden hair streamed out behind him as he let out a fierce cry and then dropped to his knees at the last moment. He skidded across the floor as the lion pounced straight over him—its massive arms closing around nothing but air. There was another fierce growl, but before it could turn around Gabriel's hands lifted into the air, finally securing his elusive hold.

A pitiful screech suddenly rang through the air. Followed by the far deeper bellows of a man. Like flipping a switch the animal melted away, leaving behind a twitching, panting man.

"Please," he wrapped his arms around his stomach, and doubled over at the waist, "please make it stop!"

Gabriel stared down at him coldly. He hadn't been programmed with the concept of mercy. Neither had he been programmed to easily forgive. But his new friends had influenced him in more ways than he cared to admit. They hadn't killed their targets. Why should he?

His fingers twitched, aching to end the job, but he didn't. Instead, he waved his hand in the air, and the shield went soaring across the loft, knocking the man unconscious. A quick glance around showed that his friends had made short work of the other two. Julian's ice man was sitting in the corner with his hands tied behind his back, and a paper take-out bag over his head, while Devon's cheetah was dangling from a rope tied to the ceiling.

STARING AT THE FUTURE

93

Gabriel eyed the acrobatic prison without a word, then he pursed his lips and turned to Devon speculatively. "A bit dramatic, don't you think?"

Devon flashed him a grin, his cheeks flushed with the thrill of the fight. "No more dramatic than fighting a lion."

Fair point.

The adrenaline faded for a moment then came back in full as Gabriel's eyes darted around the loft, searching for a door. Julian pointed to the corner and he took off sprinting at full speed, his feet echoing lightly on the tiled floor.

He didn't have the patience to open the door. Instead, he ripped it straight off its hinges, tossing it to the side then growing abruptly cautious as he stepped over the threshold.

"Natasha?" His voice was quiet, uncertain. "Are you in here? Are you okay?"

It took his eyes a second to adjust to the light, then he saw her. Looking exactly as he had remembered. Tear-stained cheeks and a look of permanent terror as she gazed up in the dark.

"...Gabriel?"

He was holding her the next second. One arm wrapped tightly around her shivering body as the other made short work of the ropes binding her hands.

"It's going to be okay," he murmured, pressing his lips to the top of her head as she huddled against his chest, "I've got you. It's all over now. We're going home."

Chapter 9

"NATASHA?" GABRIEL KNOCKED lightly on the bathroom door, feeling somehow more uncertain than he had at any point during the battle. "Honey, I don't...are you okay?"

The hesitation was unusual for him. As were the pet names. But absolutely nothing going on in the little hotel room was remotely normal. When that man had shed his skin and turned into a lion, they left normal far behind.

"Is everything all right?" Devon came up behind him with a low murmur, his bright eyes fixed on the door. "She's been in there for over an hour. What's she doing?"

Gabriel's jaw clenched impatiently, frustrated not with Natasha but at his own inability to help. "How am I supposed to know?"

Devon glanced behind him and cocked his head towards the door. "Jules, check and see."

Julian closed the magazine he'd been reading, and pushed stiffly to his feet. "You want me to use my ink to spy on a traumatized woman in the bathroom?" The others nodded at him hopefully, but he shot them down with a simple, "No."

At this point, Gabriel was severely tempted to force him to do it anyway, but at that very moment the door opened and Natasha stepped outside. Her skin was flushed yet pale, and she was staring at the trio of men standing before her with an expression Gabriel had never seen before. One that didn't at all fit the girl he remembered. One that was shy, almost scared.

He pulled in a quick breath, then took a step forward. "Hey, you." Again, he found himself on uncertain footing. His arms lifted automatically to embrace her, then dropped quickly back to his sides. "We ordered some food. Thought you might be hungry."

STARING AT THE FUTURE

Behind him, a tray of room service stood untouched in the center of the room. Her eyes flickered to it before returning to Gabriel. They rested there for a moment, then flashed just as swiftly to each of his friends.

"Natasha, this is Julian Decker and Devon Wardell." Gabriel introduced them both with a quick wave of his hand, keeping his eyes locked on her all the while. "I'm sure you recognize their faces from...well, from everything we've been doing these last... uh, while."

Since the unlikely couple had started probing through Gabriel's memories she had seen all his friends several hundred times, in several hundred different scenarios. Truth be told, she probably knew quite a bit more about them than they cared to admit themselves.

Not that it seemed to matter. The girl had completely shut down.

Much to Gabriel's supreme relief, the others made no move to approach her. They read her cagey body language like pros and kept a careful distance instead, flashing her warm smiles of welcome without making any move to come closer and shake hands.

"It's a pleasure to meet you," Julian said gently, easing the tension with that soft-spoken reassurance the others had come to expect. "I'm so sorry as to the circumstances..."

"We were all wondering what was making Gabriel stay so long in New York," Devon added with a twinkling smile. "Now we know."

Natasha shivered slightly and wrapped her arms around her chest, a little overwhelmed with the outpouring of support from strangers. She had yet to say a word since they got to the hotel a little over an hour ago, and though the ball was in her court she was at a total loss.

"I don't..." She trailed off, cringing reflexively away from the three tall men standing before her. "What I mean to say is..." For the second time, her throat closed and she fell short. Her eyes flickered once or twice to Gabriel, but when he slid his arm supportively around her waist she looked anything but comforted. In fact, the reassuring gesture seemed to send her into a new level of silent panic. "The men who took me...are they dead?"

The arm disappeared as the hotel room went abruptly silent. A clock ticked loudly on the wall as the three men looked at each other. But the tables had suddenly turned, and now they were the ones who didn't know what to say.

There was no telling how someone would react to a kidnapping. Despite their rather different upbringings, it was a lesson that their collective training had required each of them to learn very early on. The human mind would go to impossible lengths to protect itself—whether it be in compartmentalization and denial, open rebellion, or simply shutting down.

Natasha seemed to have landed somewhere amidst the three. Normally, a victim's state of mind would be rather easy to read, but the gang wasn't used to dealing with civilians. They had been trained at the highest of levels, and their opponents matched that caliber. In short, they had very little experience with people who had very little experience.

The fact that Natasha was a computer programmer with no training, context, or history with open violence? It made predicting her next moves very difficult indeed.

"I'm sorry," Gabriel stalled for time, "the men who took you—"

"Are they dead?" A strange emotion flashed through Natasha's eyes, one the others couldn't begin to understand. "Did you kill them?"

Julian shot Gabriel an uneasy glance while Devon kept his eyes on Natasha, watching her carefully. It was impossible to guess which answer she wanted to hear. In the end, the most they could do was tell her the truth.

"We didn't kill them," Gabriel said quietly, "but they're going to be staring at the inside of a jail cell for the rest of their lives. I *swear* to you," he threw caution to the wind and took her hand, staring deep into her eyes, "you're never going to see them again."

A profound silence followed this remark. One that she internalized as the others watched with bated breath. For a second, the entire room went very still. Then the strangest thing happened. Her troubled face cleared with a look of unmistakable relief.

"So, they're alive?" she repeated hopefully, unable to keep a note of desperate urgency from her voice. "All of them? You didn't...you didn't kill any of them?"

A faint frown flickered across Devon's face, but he said nothing as Gabriel took a step forward—blocking the others from sight. "You didn't want us to?"

Natasha froze. Froze so still, that for a moment the others thought that she was about to faint. Then her shoulders wilted with a little sigh as she shook her head at the floor. "I didn't want anyone to die because of me."

STARING AT THE FUTURE   97

Three pairs of eyes shot in different directions as the men quickly looked away. Three handsome faces melted with unspeakable sympathy as the frightened girl trembled before them.

That was the last that anyone talked for a while.

Julian and Devon had booked an adjoining room, so for the next few hours Gabriel and Natasha were left in peace. They went through the motions of an evening, even though it was coming up on three in the morning. Taking showers—separately and silently. Pushing the food on the room service tray around the plate. Trying to piece themselves back together, and generally acting like strangers, until Natasha suddenly broke the silence.

"Hey."

Gabriel looked up in surprise. She was standing at the foot of the bed, still wearing nothing but a towel from her recent shower. A cloud of steam rushed in from the bathroom, tinting gold in the dim light of a single lamp as she reached down and pulled him to his feet.

"Hey, yourself."

He glanced down at their joined hands, too wound up to do anything but stare. For the last few hours, he'd been trying so hard to keep his distance. To give her space. Whatever she needed, he was prepared to do. He just hadn't anticipated she'd want to do this.

"So, I realized I never said thank you." She ran her hands up over his shoulders, her wide eyes fixed on his lips. "For saving my life."

She stretched up on her toes, closing her eyes for a kiss, but he held back, catching her chin gently between his fingers and angling her face to look into his eyes.

"Thank you?" he repeated incredulously. "Natasha...this entire thing, everything that's happened to you...it's *my* fault. In what world would you possibly be thanking me?"

She hesitated for a split second, then her lips curved up in a wide smile. "Let me show you..."

She stretched up a second time, but he pulled away again, catching her hands as they started fiddling with the buttons on his shirt.

"Honey, I'm serious. When I found out Stryder had taken you, I couldn't even..." His face paled, and his eyes tightened as he remembered. "I couldn't even breathe."

A sudden silence fell between them and he bowed his head, staring unblinkingly at the floor as the weight of the world crashed down on his shoulders.

"When I came into your life, I brought all of this with me," he said quietly, stroking her knuckles with his thumbs. "I knew better. I can never tell you how sorry—"

"Hey," she interrupted loudly. "I don't want to hear it." She wrenched her hands out of his, glaring defiantly as he stared down in surprise. "It's in the past, all right? It's done. I don't want to think about it anymore, and I certainly don't want to talk about it. Not right now. Not when there are better things for us to be talking about."

Gabriel nodded quickly, surprised at her bluntness, but trying to follow along. He'd seen enough kidnapped people to have learned to go with the flow. And he'd been taken enough times himself to know there was no predicting how you might feel in those first few hours.

"Better things?" he repeated, those green eyes sparkling curiously as they stared down into hers. "And what might those be?"

Every trace of doubt and hesitation vanished from her face as she gazed up at him with a bold smile. Those hands were back. Trailing down the front of his chest. "You fought a lion for me."

His body stiffened, then froze dead still as he stared down at her in horror. "You knew he turned into a lion? He *shifted* in front of you?"

She blanched immediately, realizing her mistake, but there was no talking him down.

A wave of indescribable fury crashed over him and he took her by the shoulders, leaning down so she was forced to look directly into his eyes. "Please tell me...tell me he didn't—" The words caught in his throat and he swallowed them down, fighting hard for every breath. "Tell me they didn't touch you." A look of quiet desperation filled his face, freezing his very heart as he waited for her reply. But Natasha was having none of it. In fact, she was done talking altogether.

"Nope, and they're not the only ones..."

Gabriel sucked in a quick breath, staring down at her in utter confusion. "I'm sorry...*what*?"

STARING AT THE FUTURE

99

She backed a step away from him, lowering herself seductively onto the bed. "I told you that I don't want to talk about it. You *know* what I want to do. So, what are you waiting for?"

It took Gabriel a second to switch tracks. One minute, they'd been talking about her recent abduction and whether the men who'd done it had attacked her in the process. The next, she was slowly loosening her towel and inviting him to bed.

"I don't..." He trailed off nervously as she caught his hand, pulling him closer. The towel was lying on the floor, leaving not a stitch of clothing on her naked body. "Natasha, trust me, you don't want to do this right now. Take it from someone who's been there before—"

"Yeah, yeah, your tragic freakin' past." She scowled a moment before looking him up and down. Slow enough to make him fidget. Long enough to make him blush. Her eyes lingered on certain parts as the frustration melted into a brazen grin. "You want me, right?"

His cheeks flushed self-consciously as his gaze lowered to the floor. "You know I do."

She leaned back onto her elbows with a grin, her entire naked body on display. "Then come and get me."

There was a split second of indecision, then all hell broke loose.

She didn't wait for him to respond. Instead she leapt to her feet, throwing herself at him with the ferocity of a wild animal. He caught her with a gasp, stumbling back a step as she hitched her legs roughly around his waist. The shirt was the first to go. She ignored the buttons entirely and simply ripped it off his skin, dropping it in a pile on the floor. The pants were soon to follow.

"Are you sure about this?" he panted, trying to keep up with her manic shifts of momentum as she shoved him down onto the bed. "You don't want a little time—"

His voice cut off with a quiet gasp as she leapt on top of him, straddling his waist, her honey-colored hair spilled all over his chest.

"Stop. Talking."

Her kisses were aggressive and unfocused. Her hands pulled at his golden hair with a strength he didn't know she had. At one point, he actually pulled away as her teeth pierced his lip, but she simply laughed, and they continued like it hadn't happened.

It wasn't until there was a sharp knock on the door that they came to a sudden pause. At least one of them did. The other seemed perfectly content to keep going.

"Hold on," he murmured, pushing her back as gently as he could. Not that it made much difference—the girl was insatiable. "Just a second!"

"Sorry to bother you guys," Devon's voice called back. "But something's...come up."

Gabriel started looking around for his clothes but Natasha just grinned, pushing him back against the headboard as she started trailing kisses down his chest.

"Don't get up, baby. Not now."

He glanced down, but found himself oddly grateful for the momentary reprieve. "He wouldn't have called if it wasn't important. Just give me a second to get this sorted out."

She rolled onto her back, gazing up at him with a wicked smile. "We could always just ask him to join us..."

Gabriel's hands froze dead still as he glanced down in surprise. His pants were hanging loose around his hips, but for a moment he was too unsettled to do anything other than stare.

She's not serious...is she? She couldn't possibly—

"Wow." She brought her knees up to her chest with a mischievous giggle, waving the remains of his shirt like a tattered flag of truce. "You have *got* to lighten up!"

His body relaxed the slightest degree as he forced a strained laugh, leaning down to give her a quick kiss on the forehead. "I'll be right back."

A few seconds later—and wishing very much that he still had a shirt—he slipped through the door to the adjacent room, shutting it softly behind him. It took his eyes a second to adjust to the bright light. Another second after that to make sense of the shocked expressions in front of him.

"Dude, what happened to your face?"

Devon and Julian pushed to their feet at the same time as Gabriel cast a sideways glance at the hotel mirror. The first thing he noticed was his hair, tangled around his head in an Einstein-esque golden cloud. The second thing he noticed were the five giant scratch marks running down the side of his

STARING AT THE FUTURE

face—courtesy of an angry lion. Torn open anew by his vigorous extracurricular activities and bleeding freely down the side of his neck.

"Please tell me that was the lion," Devon joked as he walked into the bathroom and tossed Gabriel a dampened washcloth. "Otherwise we might need to have the safe sex talk."

Gabriel caught the cloth and pressed it to his cheek without a word. Strangely enough, it wasn't the lion scratches that bothered him so much—it was the bleeding. Hadn't she noticed it was happening? Wasn't she the least bit bothered? The least bit concerned?

"What's going on?" he asked evasively, shelving all those internal questions for a later time. "What's happened?"

"The future went blank," Julian said without preamble. "Stryder must already know that Natasha's gone, and he's planning the retaliation himself."

"We didn't vet this place in the slightest," Devon added, almost apologetically. "We just slipped in here to get her off the street. If they have a tracker...we'll be an easy mark."

Gabriel nodded, needing no further explanation. Now that they'd attacked Stryder head-on, it was only a matter of time before he struck back. And whenever that was going to happen, it was imperative that Natasha couldn't be anywhere in the vicinity.

He couldn't risk losing her. Not again.

...the first time had left her damaged enough.

As if sensing his thoughts Julian spoke up gently, his dark eyes flickering occasionally to the door. "How is she?"

"She's fine," Gabriel answered automatically. A flawless delivery but his answer wasn't fooling anyone, not even himself. He glanced at the door as well, a worried crease settling between his eyes. "She's...different. I don't know how else to say it."

Julian nodded thoughtfully as Devon offered a sympathetic look. "She's been to Hell and back. With no training or experience to fall back on. I can't even imagine the things that must be going through her head right now..."

"Give her a little time," Julian added softly. "If she needs normalcy, give it to her. If it's something less predictable than that...try to go with it."

Gabriel nodded sadly, his lips twitching up in a tight smile. "Speaking from experience?"

Julian laughed quietly. "Your sister isn't the easiest person to live with..."

Devon gathered up his wallet and phone, slipping them into his jacket pocket. "We'll grab a taxi and meet you out front. Head to a hotel on the other side of town."

Gabriel nodded swiftly, moving back to the door. "We'll be down in a minute."

"Sounds good. And Gabriel?"

He was already turning the lock when Devon called out to him once more, a little smile dancing around the corner of his lips.

"Maybe find yourself a shirt?"

NATASHA DIDN'T SEE the need to move, but she seemed to trust their judgement. She fell asleep on Gabriel's shoulder the second they got into the cab, and by the time they located and booked a new hotel the sun was just coming up over the tops of the trees.

"I don't see why we don't just head to the airport," Julian said quietly. "Get on a plane back to London. The three of us can come back later—deal with Stryder on our own."

Gabriel sighed as he stepped into the elevator, pushing the button for the top floor. There had been no rooms left available, so the four of them had purchased a penthouse suite. A little too close quarters for comfort, but under the circumstances they were glad for the proximity. "I thought of that..."

That was understating it. The idea had plagued him every waking moment since Natasha was safely back in his arms. Why wouldn't he bring her home to England? Safe and sound a continent away. A literal ocean between her and his enemies. But no matter which way he looked at the situation, one thing remained the same.

He would have to leave her. And that was something he was unwilling to do.

"...but it involves a goodbye." Julian finished his thought with a knowing look, glancing up at the numbers lighting across the top of the elevator. "I feel the same way every time I have to leave Angel. Especially now—"

He caught himself quickly, but Gabriel glanced over with a frown.

STARING AT THE FUTURE

"What does that mean? *Especially now—*"

"Gabriel?"

He glanced down at once, to see Natasha gazing up at him with a disoriented smile on her face. She'd passed out almost immediately in the cab, and he'd been carrying her ever since. At least five fellow patrons had swooned just at the sight of them in the lobby.

"Hey, you." He leaned down with a grin and kissed the tip of her nose. "We're at a new hotel in Manhattan. We should be safe here for a while. You can get some sleep."

She glanced uselessly around the elevator, trying to get her bearings. "Where in Manhattan? Near the park, or closer to—"

"We're not going to be staying here long," Devon interrupted casually, his bright eyes making a quick study of her face. "And I doubt we'll be going outside. This is just a stopgap until we can figure out our next step."

She glanced at him quickly then nodded, retreating farther into Gabriel's arms. "Right, of course. Sorry, I just...I'm having a little trouble keeping up."

"And that's perfectly understandable," Gabriel reassured her quickly, a slight reproach in his voice as his eyes flickered to Devon. "Things will settle down once you get a bit of sleep. I promise, this will all look different in the morning."

"Sleep," she echoed doubtfully, folding her arms across her chest with a little shiver. "I don't think I'm going to be able to sleep anytime soon."

The sentiment was sound, but there's only so much trauma the human body can take before it simply shuts down in exhaustion. Natasha was out cold before her head even hit the pillow. Gabriel tucked the covers around her, then went back out to his friends.

They gathered together in the living room for a while, throwing around different ideas and strategies before fatigue hit each one of them in turn, and they retreated to separate rooms to sleep as well. Gabriel opened the door quietly and slipped underneath the covers beside Natasha—curling his body protectively around hers as his eyes fluttered shut.

When he woke up, a few hours later, she was gone.

His hand groped the empty sheets for a minute as his heart started racing with instant panic. A cold sweat broke out over his body and he was right about to call for help, when he heard her tinkling laugh echoing from the next room.

Get a grip, man. She's back. She's safe. Everything's going to be fine.

But when Gabriel pulled on some clothes and wandered out into the next room, 'fine' was the last way he'd describe what he saw.

Natasha was there all right. But she didn't remotely resemble the girl he'd come to know.

Black leather corset. Tight fitting pants. Heels he didn't think his beloved ballerina could possibly walk in, and a storm of makeup and accessories to match.

She was splayed out across the sofa, reclining in such a suggestive position that the others had automatically settled themselves on opposite sides of the room, just to create a little casual distance. They looked up in relief when Gabriel walked in then quickly retreated to the kitchen, spared the awkward task of having to force more conversation.

"Morning," he said mildly, looking her up and down before settling himself on the opposite couch. "I see someone did a little shopping."

Her skin flushed with pride as she surveyed her new wares, seemingly oblivious to how uncomfortable they were making every other man in the room. "I hope you don't mind. You had some cash in your wallet, and I couldn't wear the same thing as yesterday."

"Not at all," Gabriel said quickly. He stared at her for a second longer before flashing a quick smile. "Have you eaten yet? We could order some room service."

"We were right about to do that." She flashed the others a smile before tossing a menu she'd been fiddling with into Gabriel's hands. "What do you say? Four coffees, four pancakes with bacon?"

Gabriel nodded automatically, glancing up in sudden surprise. "I thought you didn't like coffee. You only got that machine for me."

Her face froze a moment, then she threw back her head with a quick laugh. One that seemed just as forced as Gabriel's smile. "Yeah, most days. But I need the caffeine now. At any rate, it's nice to indulge once in a while."

She gave him a wink that was returned with a tight smile. One that didn't entirely reach his eyes. "Sure. Jules, can you call it down?"

Julian hopped down off the counter, crossing the room to the phone. "Yeah."

STARING AT THE FUTURE

"You know," Gabriel was still staring at her with that strange smile, never letting her out of his sight, "I can't remember where you even got that thing. Remind me?"

For the second time, she froze. Her pale face standing in stark contrast to the bright red she'd painted all over her lips. "Um...it was just over at—"

"Son of a bitch!"

They both looked over as Devon cursed under his breath, dropping something heavy onto the kitchen table in disgust. A closer look revealed it to be a tiny pink baby monitor, the one he'd set up in Aria's room to watch over her when he was away.

"What's wrong with it?" Gabriel asked, pushing off the sofa and coming over for a better look. "Besides the color and the helicopter-parenting vibes?"

Devon ignored his jabs completely, giving the monitor another useless shake. "It got fried in Molly's electrical storm. I've got audio, but no image."

A peculiar look flashed across Gabriel's face, and he gestured over his shoulder with a sudden smile. "Let Natasha take a look at it."

Devon glanced up in surprise. "Her?"

Natasha was similarly startled. "Me?"

"Of course you," Gabriel said easily, rewarding her look of alarm with a deceptively charming smile. "No need to be modest, sweetheart. Natasha's a tech genius. She'll have that working in no time."

"Oh yeah?" Devon turned to her hopefully, offering the broken device. "That would be great. I'd really appreciate it."

She pushed slowly off the couch, dragging her feet as she made her way reluctantly into the kitchen. "Don't, uh...don't mention it. I'd be happy to look."

The men watched as she grabbed the broken monitor, turning it over and over in her hands. A look of intense concentration clouded across her face as she tried half-heartedly pushing at a few buttons, wiping off the charcoaled surface in defeat.

"I'm afraid it got hit pretty hard," she said with a sympathetic wince, setting it back down where she'd found it. "I don't think there's anything I can do without my tools."

Devon nodded quickly and didn't look too surprised. Gabriel, on the other hand, was staring across the table like he was seeing the beautiful girl for the very first time.

"That's a real shame," he said quietly, pushing slowly to his feet. "If only Hans were here, maybe he'd have some ideas."

She fell back as he moved towards her, trying desperately to maintain a smile. "Hans?" Her voice was higher than usual, strained and tight. "Oh, yeah... I guess that he would."

Gabriel nodded with that same smile. "Maybe we should call him."

She backed into the coffee table, tripping with surprise as she hastened to move around it instead. "Sure, but...can we call him after breakfast? My head's really dizzy, and—"

In a flash, Gabriel was across the room—moving with a predatory speed and grace that left Natasha time for only a single scream. The next second he smashed her head against the table, stepping back with a dark look as she fell unconscious at his feet.

"Gabriel! What the hell are you doing?!" Devon shouted, blurring across the suite as he knelt to take her pulse.

A second later Julian walked back into the room, freezing in sudden astonishment as he finished with the breakfast order and hung up the phone. "What the... What just happened?!"

"He knocked her out," Devon answered in disbelief, propping her up against the sofa as he hastened to check all other vitals. "Gave her a severe concussion. We need to get her—"

"Don't bother."

Both men looked up in shock as Gabriel folded his arms across his chest—staring down at the fallen girl with the coldest expression either of his friends had ever seen.

"That's not Natasha."

Chapter 10

"WAKE HER UP."

There wasn't an ounce of feeling in Gabriel's voice as he stared down at her. Not a hint of compassion for the girl he had spent the night with. The one who had pulled him into her bed.

"Gabriel, are you sure about this?" Devon glanced down nervously at the girl—a girl he'd tied up himself through a creative use of bed sheets. "I mean, she was kidnapped. It's no wonder she's acting a little strange—"

"It's. Not. Her." Gabriel lifted his eyes for only a moment, leveling Devon squarely in his gaze. "Wouldn't you know if it wasn't Rae?"

It was the first time he'd made the comparison. At least out loud. Just the fact that he'd done so had a more profound effect on the others than anything else that had happened thus far.

Devon nodded slowly and pulled out a lighter, setting the corner of a cloth napkin aflame before quickly putting it out with his hand. He held the cloth beneath her nose, letting the smoke waft over her bloody face. Julian silently disconnected the fire alarm.

It took a second to work. Then there was a soft moan as she shook her head from side to side. When she was unable to move the rest of her body her eyes fluttered open, taking a second to focus before dilating in sudden fear. "Gabriel?" She tugged against at her restraints, staring up at him with all the innocence of a young martyr betrayed by the people sworn to protect. "What's going on?"

It was an admirable performance. One that Gabriel almost believed himself. But the longer she sat there, staring up at him with those wide, beautiful eyes, the more he wondered how he'd ever been fooled. Even for a second.

This was not his precious Natasha. This girl was the farthest thing from.

"You're going to have to help me out here." He knelt in front of her, not a shred of leniency in his handsome face. "See...I don't know what to call you."

Only an expert would have been able to detect the split-second of hesitation before she spoke again. The fleeting look of panic that broke through her self-righteous mask.

"What to call...I have no idea what you're talking about!" Instead of focusing on Gabriel she turned her attention to the others, casting them looks of open terror as she silently begged for their help. "What's the matter with him?! He knows my name! You all do!"

It was a heart-wrenching plea, but it fell on deaf ears. The gang had known each other long enough to trust each other completely. Even if that meant sitting idly by while their friend did the inconceivable. Even if it meant turning a blind eye to the tears of a helpless girl.

"You're good." Gabriel flashed a humorless smile. "Very good. I can see why Stryder picked you. But playtime's over. This is the part where you start answering my questions or things become very unpleasant, very fast. Do you understand?"

"Gabriel, *please*!" Tears streamed freely down her face as she stretched out her tied hands as far as they would go. "It's me. You *know* it's me! It's Natasha!"

The words echoed in the little room, dying in the air between them. For a moment, neither person moved. She sat there, bound and crying, while Gabriel stared back impassively.

Then the tears stopped, and her lips twitched up with a little smile. "Give me a break. I never met the girl." She tossed back her hair and straightened up against the couch. "You try impersonating someone you know nothing about."

Julian let out a quiet gasp of disbelief, but Gabriel pushed to his feet with a wry smile. He was neither surprised nor particularly upset. His mind was focused on a solitary thing.

"Where's Natasha?" He felt like he'd been asking the question for the better part of his life. Even before he'd met her, a part of him had always been searching for this girl.

She grinned again, cocking her head mischievously to the side as she stared up at him with a dimpled smile. "She's right here in front of you. You didn't like the little performance she gave last night?"

For the first time, a flicker of true anger broke through Gabriel's carefully controlled mask. He knelt again, bringing them to eye level, while he spoke in a deadly calm. "I'm afraid you may be under some misconceptions as to what

STARING AT THE FUTURE

exactly is going on here, and how far I'm willing to go. Allow me to rid you of those notions."

Moving with an exaggerated slowness, he brought his hand up between them. Then, one by one, he curled his fingers into a fist. The girl flinched, preparing to get hit, but she had no way of knowing what was going to happen next. No way of knowing that Gabriel had no intention of using an instrument as blunt and predictable as his fists. No way of knowing that he had a far more dangerous weapon hiding up his sleeve.

The second his last finger came down, an indescribable wave of pain shot through her entire body. Burning her alive. As if her blood itself was suddenly on fire. Her head flew back and she let out an ear-splitting scream. One that bounced in ghastly echoes off the polished tile.

Then, as quickly as it started, it was over. The room filled with a chilling silence, one that was interrupted only by the girl's frantic breathing as she waited for the next round.

"Let's start with something simple," Gabriel said quietly. He alone hadn't flinched at the sound of her scream. In fact, he seemed depressingly used to it. "Shift back."

For once, the girl didn't come back with some wise-ass remark. No sarcastic retort. She simply stared at him for a moment, her eyes flickering down to his hands, before the air around her shimmered and the beautiful girl sitting in front of them melted away. She was replaced with someone a little curvier, a little taller. Dark eyes, painted lips, and a long mane of brunette hair.

Gabriel watched the transformation without blinking, watched as the girl he cared about above all others was replaced with a conniving snake. "What's your name?"

"Bianca."

Her voice was different, too. It was breathy. Girly. The kind of voice that reminded Gabriel strangely of the three girls they'd met on the train.

"Well, *Bianca*...I'll ask you again." He deliberately flexed his fingers before doing so, staring deep into her eyes. "Where's Natasha?"

Her entire face changed upon hearing the name, panicked to the point of making her physically sick. For a second her eyes flickered once more to his friends, but finding no help there they returned to Gabriel with the hint of a plea. "He'll kill me if I tell you."

"And I'll kill you right now if you don't," Gabriel assured her. It was impossible to doubt the sincerity in his voice, and she let out a little whimper. "I have no idea why you were sent here in the first place, what sick game you're playing, but I don't—"

"Stryder didn't want to give up on you," she said quickly, desperately relieved to be talking about anything that wasn't the location of the elusive Natasha. "He holds you as some golden standard. The pinnacle of what inked people can achieve."

Gabriel stared back without a shred of emotion. "How sweet."

"The three of you were never supposed to be together," she continued, casting glances at the others. "But since you were, I was supposed to find out whatever information I could and pass it back to him."

"How?" Devon asked sharply, intervening for the first time.

Her face fell miserably as she glanced out the window towards the park. "Through channels..."

It was a vague response, one that made way for a million questions, but before Devon could step up and ask Gabriel shut it down with three simple words.

"I don't care."

The interrogation came to an abrupt standstill. Both parties fell instinctively quiet as he leaned forward once again, his voice sending chills up the prisoner's arms.

"Where's Natasha?"

A stream of silent tears spilled down her face as she stared wretchedly up at him.

"...he will *kill* me."

Gabriel nodded slowly, but in his eyes there wasn't a drop of pity. "You're a fool if you think I won't do the same. I guarantee, I've left a bigger body count in my wake than Stryder. I think you know that. And I'm tired of asking the question."

The girl let out a broken sob and bowed her head. Unable to reconcile the fact that the man who'd shown her love and kindness the previous night could possibly be worse than the monster she'd known her entire life. Unable to see him as the greater of two evils.

STARING AT THE FUTURE 111

A flash of impatience shot through Gabriel's eyes, but just as he raised his hand, the deadly ink rising to the surface of his skin, a more gentle hand pulled him back. He pushed to his feet in exasperation, turning around to see Julian staring steadily back at him.

"Jules, now is *not* the—"

"You don't need to ask the question again, and she doesn't need to answer it." Julian spoke quickly and quietly, a practiced calm against his friend's wrath. "All we need is her face."

It took Gabriel a moment to understand. A moment to see the brilliant simplicity in what his friend was suggesting. A flicker of hope broke through the anger driving him, and for a split-second that callous chill thawed away to the point of a smile.

"Shift back." He tossed the command over his shoulder, pulling out his phone at the same time. "Shift back to Natasha."

Bianca froze in confusion, looking from one man to the next. "Why do you—"

"Just do it," Devon advised softly.

A minute later, all four of them were sitting on the couch. Just as normal as if they were settling in to watch a long movie. Granted, one of them had a gun pressed between her ribs, but that wasn't something you could exactly see from the phone.

"I still can't believe that you and Kraigan Facetime," Devon muttered in disbelief. He shifted uneasily on the cushions, pressed between Bianca and Julian.

Gabriel dialed the number, and shot him a sideways glance as the phone rang. "I can't believe you two don't. He's technically your brother, after all."

"*Half*-brother. *In-law*."

"A brother's a brother."

Julian stifled a grin as Devon full-on shuddered.

"Don't say that," he hissed, lowering his voice as if they could already be heard. "It's like if you came home to find your parents had adopted a rabid dog. Can't we just agree to *never* talk about it? Pretend like it didn't happen? Keep it outside?"

Julian tilted his head back with a faint smile, somehow still able to see the humor in things despite the bizarre nature of what they were about to do. "I wonder if that means that Camille is eventually going to be your sister.

And to think, when the two of you first met she was about two seconds away from—*hey*...Kraigan?"

His voice turned up into an automatic question, and it was easy to see why. The last time the others had seen Rae's deplorable half-brother, he had been standing in front of the London City Hall loudly proffering his services as a hit man, while simultaneously skimming money from the children's hospital fundraising just next door.

The man on the other end of the phone was a different story.

"Julian?! Devon?!" Kraigan's face brightened with delight as he leaned back against his pool chair sipping an afternoon Mai-Tai as the English sun went down. "Well, this is certainly a surprise! How are you guys doing?! It's been such a long time!"

"Not long enough..." Julian muttered, too quiet to hear. Devon simply stared in open-mouthed shock, unable to tear his eyes away from the argyle sweater-vest.

"Hey, buddy, we actually don't have a lot of time." Gabriel leaned forward with a tight smile, flashing the phone to Bianca sitting there with Natasha's lovely face. "I need you to track this girl for me. Can you see her okay? The image is clear?"

"Uh...yeah, but..." Kraigan's mouth twitched up in a quirky grin. "You want me to track her? She's sitting right there."

Gabriel returned the question with a steady smile. "Humor me..."

A second later, they had an address. One that was rather close to where they were staying in Manhattan. Kraigan wished them all a 'happy hunt' and then clicked off his phone, off to fire up the nightly barbeque. Devon stalked away, assumedly to reevaluate his entire life, as Julian began gathering up their things to move yet again. Leaving Gabriel sitting on the couch with the girl who had been pretending to be his missing girlfriend.

"I'm sorry," she whispered, melting back into her original form as an errant tear fell down her cheek. "I never meant to...I mean, I *did*, but..." She stared up at him, silently hoping for him to understand. "It was just following orders, you know?"

He stared down at the couch for a moment before lifting his head to look at her. All the pretenses, threats, and emotions fell away—and for a second it was just *them*. Then a hard look flashed through his eyes, and he slowly shook his head. "Not all of it."

Before she could answer his hand shot out at the speed of light, catching her full in the face. As it turned out, he could use his fists after all. Her head slumped down onto her chest as he pushed briskly to his feet ready to leave the entire mess behind him. "Jules, can you get her out of here?"

The psychic paused his packing, glancing over at the unconscious girl. On the one hand, he seemed relieved that Gabriel was delegating the responsibility rather than just giving in to his darker inclinations and killing her outright. On the other hand, a nagging question hovered on the tip of his tongue, troubling his dark eyes.

"Sure. Just give me a second." He started heading into one of the bedrooms before pausing suddenly and glancing back. "Gabriel, you didn't...I mean, you didn't actually..."

Gabriel's eyes burned as they locked onto the sleeping girl. "Just get her out of here."

THE GIRL WAS LEFT IN the middle of Central Park. Tied to a bench. A note taped to her chest.

Better Luck Next Time

If the men had the luxury of time they might have been able to come up with a more creative option, but the clock was ticking and there wasn't a moment to lose.

The address Kraigan had given them wasn't a warehouse, like the place where they'd found Bianca; it was actually a store front. A place that claimed to have had something to do with selling women's raincoats, but was now closed due to renovations.

The men waited until nightfall then approached it head-on, dropping silently through the skylight and landing without a noise on the carpeted floor. There wasn't a guard in sight. No barrage of jungle predators lying in wait. Just a single man watching television from a room in the back, snacking loudly on leftover Chinese whilst keeping his chair angled so he had a clear view of a locked door at the end of the hall.

Devon and Julian turned their eyes to the man. Gabriel turned his eyes to the door.

He was on the verge of throwing caution to the wind and simply breaking it down, when Devon tapped him lightly on the shoulder and cocked his head towards the man. Rules were rules. You didn't want to rescue a victim when there was still an active target in play. Especially when that target had two handguns strapped to his waist.

Gabriel sighed, nodded, and followed the other two as they crept down the hall.

Surely there's a faster way of doing this, he thought impatiently as they stole along in the shadows. *Surely Devon could just blur over there and take him out. Or Jules could find out what sort of ink he's carrying. Or I could just kill him with my own ink right now.*

He was still contemplating different ways to end the man's life, when there was a sudden choking sound and a chair scraped back against the floor. The three men straightened up in unison and watched in surprise as the man coughed and heaved, falling to the floor with a piece of moo-shu-pork lodged in his throat.

The others froze where they stood, uncertain how to proceed, but Gabriel simply shrugged with a smile, turning on his heel to recover Natasha. It wasn't until Devon grabbed his arm again—a little chidingly this time—that he rolled his eyes and swept into the room.

By now, the man's face had turned an ugly shade of maroon. He glanced up as Gabriel walked towards him, but was unable to do anything other than gasp and heave.

"No, that's all right. Don't bother getting up."

Gabriel knelt and quickly disarmed the man of any weapons he might be carrying, tossing them down the hall towards his friends. Then he stood up, prepared to leave, when he saw said friends staring at him accusingly. "What?" he asked defensively, coming around behind and lifting the man to his feet. "I was right about to..."

In what felt like the most counterintuitive thing in the world, Gabriel wrapped his arms around the man's diaphragm and pulled with all his might, giving him an unnecessarily rough version of the Heimlich maneuver. The piece of pork went shooting to the opposite side of the room, but before the man

STARING AT THE FUTURE

could even pull in a full breath Gabriel hit him over the back of the head, felling him once more.

"Can we go now?" he demanded, wiping his hands on his jeans. "Are you satisfied?"

"Thank goodness this isn't an official mission," Julian muttered as the three of them headed back down the hall. "They'd never believe us in debrief."

They came to a stop in front of the locked door, staring at it with the caution of a group of people who'd recently spent some time in the ICU. Gabriel was about to reach for the handle, when Devon caught him by the wrist.

"Let me do it," he said quietly. "If it's a trap, my reflexes are faster."

"Debatable."

"Gabriel," Julian pulled him back as well, "let him do it. No one's deciding anything, so I can't see what's going to happen. We have no idea what's waiting on the other side of that door."

Gabriel stared a second longer at the frame then nodded curtly, stepping back to let his friend take the lead. He and Julian looked on as Devon squared his shoulders, took a deep breath, then kicked the whole thing down. It landed with a clatter in the middle of the room, the broken pieces scattering around what looked like an empty chair.

"Is she in there?" Gabriel peered around the corner, and his eyes fell on the chair with dismay. There were tiny pieces of rope on the floor around it, but they looked like they'd been chewed right through. "Dev, do you see her?"

Devon was walking inside very slowly, his fox eyes needing no time whatsoever to adjust to the dim light. He paused to examine the chair, but then a movement in the corner of the room caught his eye. A look of apprehension flickered across his face, followed immediately by protective concern as he recognized the shaking form in the corner as that of a petite girl.

"Natasha?" he asked carefully, placing a tentative hand on her shoulder. "Is that—"

"*Hi—YAH!*"

There was a gasp of surprise, followed by a muffled profanity as Devon's body went flying through the air—crashing hard into the broken pieces of the door. He let out a quiet groan as Julian and Gabriel hurried inside, staring not at their friend but at the wide-eyed girl who'd thrown him.

"*NATASHA?*"

"GABRIEL!"

The next second, they were in each other's arms. Every vestige of fear and doubt and dread fell away as they held onto each other for all their worth, gripping as hard as they dared, unable to see anything else in the world around them. It wasn't until Gabriel's head began to spin that he realized he hadn't even been breathing.

"It's really you." He pulled back, smoothing her hair as he stared deep into her eyes. Rememorizing the lines of color. That perfect ocean hue. "It's really you."

"Of course it's me," she breathed, pressing her face into his jacket and smiling as she inhaled the familiar scent. "Who else do you know can throw as well as that?"

Oh. Right.

Gabriel glanced behind him to see Devon pushing stiffly to his feet. An angry red welt was rising on his forehead, and his eyes flickered to the happy couple with a rueful scowl.

"Congratulations. She's perfect for you."

Chapter 11

"—AT WHICH POINT HE DECIDED a boat wouldn't be fast enough, so he simply threw his body off the roof."

A tinkling laugh echoed from the next room, rousing Gabriel from a deep sleep. His eyes blinked slowly open and shut. But instead of getting up to investigate, he simply rolled onto his back—staring up at the ceiling with a faint smile as he enjoyed the sound.

"But what about the caves?! You said there were—"

"Oh, there were thousands. But he insisted that, unlike the rest of the Finnish delegation, he wasn't allergic to shellfish."

Another round of raucous laughter. This time, two deeper voices joined in.

Natasha hadn't really talked to anyone except Gabriel since the other night. Not that the others expected anything more. The days spent in forced captivity had depleted her adrenaline and temporarily blunted the need to introduce more strangers into her life. She'd tripped over a trash can when Devon blurred across the hotel room, and stayed up long enough to see Julian's eyes turn white before she passed out from utter exhaustion in Gabriel's arms.

From the sounds of things, she was making up for all that now.

"So, what happened to the dirigible?" she asked in disbelief.

"He had it deflated and shipped to a storage locker in London," Julian replied with a touch of amusement. "Said he was going to save it for a rainy day..."

In the explosion of laughter that followed Gabriel pushed to his feet and pulled on the same clothes as yesterday, shaking out his hair before heading down the hall. The laughter got louder and louder the closer he got, making him smile in spite of himself. He paused just out of sight, lingering for a moment behind the corner.

For a split second, he was struck with the oddest sense of déjà vu. Hadn't he just seen this? Julian, Devon, and Natasha hanging out in the living room of yet another hotel room, in yet another part of the city he would never come to know? Less than twenty-four hours ago, he had woken up and stumbled upon an eerily similar scene. A collision of worlds he had never consciously intended to come together. A collision based upon the most dangerous kind of lie.

However, while things might have looked the same from a distance, upon closer inspection they couldn't have been more different.

To start, everyone was sitting on the floor. A small army of Chinese take-out boxes littered the carpet between them. Boxes that they passed back and forth, hardly seeming to notice as they dipped in their chopsticks and ripped open packets of sauce. Instead of keeping their distance, as the men had done instinctively with Bianca, there was something strangely familiar about the way they were clustered. Strangely uninhibited about the way they were reclining—so unguarded and relaxed. It was as if they were sitting with Molly or Angel, instead of a girl they hardly knew. In fact, if Gabriel hadn't known better, he would have guessed they were the oldest of friends. Sprawled out in pajamas and sweat pants, hair still damp from showers, laughing with mouths full of noodles as the sun rose over New York City.

...gossiping about me.

"All right, kids. Storytime's over."

They looked around to see him leaning against the wall, arms folded across his chest, the hint of a smile sparkling in his eyes. While the men seemed perfectly content to ignore him Natasha leapt to her feet the instant their eyes met, racing across the room.

"How come you never told me that you pretended to be an air traffic controller to gain access to a military stronghold on the coast of Greece?"

Gabriel blinked slowly as she skidded to a stop in front of him. "And good morning to you."

She continued as if he hadn't spoken, bouncing with the uncontrollable energy of someone who was indulging in vast amounts of caffeine for the first time in days. "Julian said they were considering naming a zoo after you."

Gabriel's eyes flickered over her head, landing with faint accusation on his friend. Julian grinned, but had the decency to blush as he quickly busied himself with his noodles.

"They do that with everybody. It wasn't just me."

STARING AT THE FUTURE

Natasha raised her eyebrows slowly, pursing her lips as her arms folded playfully across her chest. "And Devon said that the only reason you were there in the first place was to break into a prison. The same prison where you were later incarcerated."

Devon had no shame. Just a brazen grin. The opportunity for half a decade's worth of karma had just landed in his lap, and he wasn't about to let it slip away.

"Yeah, well," Gabriel wrapped his arm around Natasha's shoulders, pulling her in for a quick kiss on the lips, "you'll soon learn not to listen to anything Devon says. The man's a pathological liar. Julian isn't even his friend, he's his legal conservator."

She snorted in laughter, and he pulled her tighter against his chest. He didn't think he would ever get over it—the novelty of simply holding her in his arms.

How was it that this one girl seemed to have nothing in common with all the rest? How had she eliminated all his other points of reference, claiming a pedestal of her own? Why did kissing her feel terrifying and thrilling and new? Like he was learning to kiss for the first time.

Whatever existential transformation was coming over him, it must have shown on his face. The others watched with secret smiles as he brushed his lips across her forehead. Shared a grin at the silent sigh of contentment as he gathered her up in his arms.

"How are you feeling?" he murmured, tilting her face to stare searchingly into her eyes. Morning banter was a good sign, but the girl had been abducted. That kind of thing never failed to leave a mark. "Do you want to—"

"I feel fine."

"You don't have to feel fine," he pressed softly. "You have every right to be—"

"Gabriel...I feel fine." She spoke quietly, but it was impossible to doubt the sincerity. Her eyes glowed as they locked onto his, lingering there for a moment before she gave his hand a gentle tug, leading him back to the others. "Come on. Get some breakfast."

In hindsight, Gabriel didn't know whether he'd call it breakfast or a crucifixion. When he'd decided to open his mind to Natasha, he'd assumed his life was an open book. But it was quickly becoming clear there were stories he'd neglected to tell her. Stories his subconscious had wisely chosen to suppress. Fortunately for her, but rather unfortunately for him, Devon and Julian seemed to remember every one of them.

"What does that mean?" she asked in astonishment, her eyes widening to cartoonish saucers on her lovely face. "*Thawed him out of the ice.*"

Julian suppressed a theatric shudder. "Exactly what it sounds like."

"All right, enough." Gabriel had tried to be a good sport, but his girlfriend imagining him as some sort of resurrected popsicle was the last straw. "It isn't like the two of you don't have stories of your own. What about that time you got shot, Jules? That was funny."

Julian's face abruptly fell, but Devon intervened with a smug smile.

"You're just lucky that hotel came with a hair dryer."

The argument probably could have gone on several rounds longer, if it weren't for the delighted burst of laughter that stopped the men in their tracks. They turned in unison to see Natasha doubled over at the waist, one hand hanging onto Gabriel for support as the other pointed viciously at his chest. Probably imagining some sort of fossilized version of him.

In a flash, all the teasing was forgotten. They watched her instead, the same little smile twinkling in their eyes as the newest member of the gang was unknowingly brought into the fold.

"Molly's going to lose her mind," Devon murmured, far quieter than the laughing girl could hear. "Dress her up like a little doll."

"Angel fought her off," Gabriel replied evenly, never taking his eyes away for even a second. "Natasha can, too."

"I'm sorry?" Upon hearing her own name, Natasha stopped laughing and tuned back in to the conversation, completely oblivious to the adorably endearing effect she'd had on everyone watching. "I can do what?"

"You can be careful," Julian interceded gracefully, gesturing to her mug of tea with a little smile. "That's about to spill."

Gabriel reached over automatically, catching it before it could fall, but Natasha ignored the mug completely, staring in wonder at Julian's clairvoyant eyes.

"That's incredible. How you do that. I can't even..." She stared at him thoughtfully for a moment before her face brightened with a sudden flicker of mischief.

STARING AT THE FUTURE 121

Gabriel looked on with amusement as Julian's head jerked up in surprise. Their eyes met for a split second—ocean blue and prophetic white—before he snapped suddenly back to the present, laughing all the while.

"Yeah, I wouldn't recommend that. Those things aren't flame resistant."

Natasha bit down on her lip, plotting on the fly. Testing out the limits of the psychic's powers with the same wide-eyed wonder as all the rest when they saw it for the first time.

Another secret decision. Another laughing warning.

"...he isn't either."

Gabriel glanced down suspiciously. "Are you talking about me?"

But Natasha was on a roll. No sooner had Julian warned her, "he'll catch it," than she froze very still. Her spine straightened as every muscle stiffened into place. Then, with a flick of her hands, she lobbed her spoon at Devon as fast as she could.

As if in slow motion, he reached up and closed his fingers around the metal. It was an automatic response and he offered it back politely, thinking it to be a mistake. It wasn't until Gabriel started laughing that he realized she had been testing him as well.

"Cute." He flicked a bit of rice in her direction, but placed the spoon back in her hands with an indulgent grin. "We're not seals, you know. We don't perform on command."

"Sorry." A blush rose in her cheeks with a breathless smile. "I've just never seen anyone with ink like yours. Like either of yours, actually. I mean, just in Gabriel's mind."

A thoughtful silence descended upon the room as the others considered this. While Gabriel might have been a special circumstance, the others had been raised the same way that most children with ink were raised. In a tightly-knit community. Constantly surrounded by their own. Their futures decided. Their paths intertwined.

"No one you grew up with had ink like this?" Julian asked curiously.

Natasha hesitated for a moment before her body stiffened with a self-conscious flush. "No one I grew up with had ink."

It was a rather strange way to end what had been a lively conversation. Devon and Julian headed out into the city to pick up some much-needed supplies, while Gabriel and Natasha took advantage of their absence to climb back into bed, curling up in each other's arms.

"So, Devon's the husband?" Natasha tilted her head with an impish smile. "I wouldn't have tried to steal his girl."

Gabriel chuckled, smoothing the back of her hair with an affectionate smile. "Yes, well, I've always been very ambitious."

"*Reckless.* Don't you mean *reckless*?" Her eyes clouded for a moment as she ran a hand along the side of his face. "You know, when Stryder pulled out all those guns at the market you were the only person in the city who didn't flinch."

Gabriel's pulse quickened, and he stifled a sigh. Not long after the others had left, Natasha had asked if she could see what had happened since that fateful morning. She'd asked in her own unique way, whispering, "No secrets?" before she held out her hands.

It had been hard on them both. Seeing the destruction that one vengeful man had wreaked upon their happy lives. Watching their world unravel with the pulling of a single thread. The news of Peter and Magda's deaths had hit Natasha especially hard. But, painful as it was, Gabriel had to admit that sharing the memories was for the best. At the very least, she had a right to know what happened. He would have given his life to have kept it from happening at all.

"I'm sorry," he murmured, so softly she could barely hear. "I'm sorry for dragging you into my world. None of this would have happened if I hadn't—"

"*Hey*," she put her hand on his with sudden conviction, "this is supposed to be my world, too. These are supposed to be my people. Devon, Julian..." Her voice trailed off as she glanced down at the sheets, looking suddenly embarrassed. "This isn't supposed to be the first time I've seen that sort of thing."

Gabriel's eyes tightened with concern, but he didn't say a word. He simply tilted her head back up to his, staring with silent reassurance as she gathered her thoughts.

"My parents kept me pretty isolated. Didn't want me to be defined by my ink. When I was two years old, they moved to New York. Wanted me to go to this great school in America."

Gabriel frowned. The two seemed counterintuitive.

"A *great* school? In *America*?"

She grinned, and smacked his arm. "You know, there are some great things in this world that don't come from England."

His face grew very serious. "Take it back."

Another smile warmed her cheeks, but it faded the longer she lay there. After a few moments, there was nothing left of it at all.

"They're really your family, aren't they?" she asked softly. "And England is your home."

Gabriel nodded cautiously. She knew all this. She'd seen it in his memories. Able to derive the future from the past. Why was she asking about it now?

"You're not going to stay in New York, are you?"

There it was.

Some men might have sugarcoated it. Some men might have panicked and stalled for time. But Gabriel had never been one of those men.

"No," he said simply. A silence rang out between them. But he didn't leave it at that. He countered with a question of his own. "Are you?"

She looked up at him in shock, a thousand things dancing behind her eyes before she bowed her head with a sudden sigh. "My stepdad lives here. I can't just leave..."

Gabriel fought back a sudden grimace, remembering for the first time. "Actually, I may have already got the ball rolling on that..."

THE TWO STAYED IN BED for the better part of an hour. Gabriel got the feeling that Devon and Julian were staying away on purpose, graciously giving them time. They kissed and cuddled, occasionally straying into something a bit more, but for the most part they were content to simply lay in each other's arms. They hadn't understood the profound need for it until it had been taken away. Hadn't understood the primal desire until they thought they'd lost it forever.

Barring any further complications, they might have happily stayed in bed several hours more if it hadn't been for a sudden but insistent knock upon the door.

"Guys? Guys, are you in there?"

The tension in Devon's voice raised the hairs on the back of Gabriel's neck, and he was out of bed before he'd even finished the question.

"Stay here," he instructed quietly, pulling on a shirt. "Let me see what's going on."

Natasha sat straight up on the bed, wrapping the sheets around her tiny shoulders with a shiver. Through the lens of her ink, she had recently seen the man standing in front of her go head-to-head with a lion. She didn't like to think what could make a guy like that nervous.

"Shouldn't I go with you?" Her voice dropped to an automatic whisper as she rifled around in her purse. "I still have my taser—"

"Honey." She looked up to see him standing right in front of her, staring down with the world's most tender smile. His hands eased the straps of the bag from her hands, setting it back on the nightstand as he leaned down to kiss her forehead. "Please just stay here."

"...okay."

A second later he was out the door, shutting it carefully behind him. Devon had called out of his own volition, which meant that he wasn't in any immediate physical harm, but the lot of them had been through so much in the last few days he wasn't ruling anything—

"Well, speak of the devil and he shall appear!"

Gabriel froze in his tracks. He knew that voice. That hacking cough. That ridiculous Southern warble. The sound of it still made him instinctively reach for a weapon.

"Eliza?"

He rounded the corner to see Canary standing in the entryway, wedged in between Julian and Devon. She looked even more ridiculous than usual, dwarfed by the two towering men, and seemed to have added at least ten new shawls to her ever-growing collection.

"Well, don't keep an old woman waiting—come here and give me a hug!" she demanded with a toothy smile. "I was just telling these two how you almost drowned in that puddle!"

Chapter 12

"I DON'T UNDERSTAND," Gabriel let himself be pulled into an effusive hug, staring in bewilderment over the top of her head at his friends. "What are you doing here?"

"We found her wandering around on the street," Devon answered, looking at the woman with a strange sort of reverence. "Apparently, she'd decided to go looking for you. Went to all the usual Brooklyn haunts. Julian's keeping an eye on those places, so..."

Gabriel didn't understand the decision. Nor the reverence. But those were both matters for a different time. Canary had been safest when she was on the other side of the state. Now that she was back, she'd have to stay with them until this whole thing was over. There was no way he was willing to risk her safety by having it any other way.

And that means...

"Well, now that you're here...want to stay for dinner?" He forced a strained smile, one that she saw through immediately.

Her face crinkled up with another wheezing cough as she smacked the center of his chest. "You know, kid, considering you're supposed to be some spy, you've got to be one of the worst liars I've ever seen."

"Don't take it personally," Devon muttered. "I get that all the time."

"Why do you want me to stay for dinner?" As old as her eyes were they sharpened to full attention, not missing a single detail. "Or, rather, why don't you want me to leave? What's been going on since I left? What have you gotten yourself in to now?" Her eyes swept over the trio, lingering on each one before narrowing with sudden suspicion. "Did you start a boy band?"

Julian snorted and looked away, whilst Devon looked like the words 'boy band' would haunt him forever. But Gabriel took a slow step forward, bracing for the worst.

"Actually, there's rather a lot I need to tell you..."

CONSIDERING THE LENGTH of the story, it didn't take all that long. Canary already knew all the Brooklyn players, and after Gabriel's in-depth confession about his past she had a pretty good sense of the London gang as well. Her eyes welled up with sudden tears when he told her about the Fischers, and her shoulders fell with a weary sigh when he got to Natasha's abduction.

"But you got her back?" she interrupted. The two were on the balcony of the penthouse apartment, clutching mugs of coffee between their shivering hands. "You wouldn't be sitting here if you hadn't gotten her back. And that means—"

"Canary?"

The pair of them whirled around as Natasha ventured tentatively onto the patio. One of the guys had obviously told her it was safe to come out, and she rushed into Eliza's arms without a thought or hesitation. The two embraced for a long moment as Gabriel looked on. So different, yet so much the same. The two most precious people in the city. Ones he had to protect.

"You're staying here with us, right?" Natasha asked without preamble. She wasn't one to easily cry, but Canary was weeping in open relief. "Until this mess is sorted, it isn't safe for you to be on your own in the city. Gabriel says—"

"Gabriel already beat you to the punch, my dear." Canary pulled back with a shaky breath, then forced a watery smile. "Although he wasn't as forthcoming. Planned on stringing it along as a series of meal invitations. Like I wouldn't notice I'd never gone home."

Gabriel blushed, but remained completely unapologetic. These women were in his care now. He would do anything he had to to keep them safe. "Come on, let's go back inside. We'll order some food."

It was truly one of the strangest dinners Gabriel had ever had. Mostly because Canary insisted that they make it some sort of family affair. She said that she wanted to 'get to know Gabriel's new friends,' and so instead of ordering something premade she forced the men to run out and get groceries so they could prepare a meal for themselves.

"*New* friends, huh?"

Gabriel and Julian were in the kitchen, opening another bottle of wine. The alcohol had been Devon's idea. A conversational lubricant that would relax the

STARING AT THE FUTURE

more vulnerable members of their party and hopefully allow them all to get a good night's sleep.

Gabriel glanced over as he picked up a corkscrew. "Yeah," he laughed shortly, "apparently you guys are the new ones."

Julian nodded with a smile, but kept his eyes on his work. He'd looked a little shaken up since the three of them got in that afternoon, much the same way Gabriel had been the first time the old woman had burst uninvited into his own life.

"So, what do you think of her?" he asked curiously, leaning back against the counter with a hidden smile. He couldn't imagine two more different people than Julian and Eliza P. Duncan.

Julian glanced up quickly, then looked away with a casual shrug. "She's, uh...she's pretty handsy."

Gabriel grinned, remembering their first encounter at the bar. The time when she'd 'accidentally' spilled her drink all over his pants, trying to keep him from getting himself killed. "Did she grope you?"

The psychic spat out a mouthful of wine. "What? *No!*" He grabbed a handful of glasses off the counter, then shot Gabriel a look of deep concern. "Why would you ask that—"

"We'd better get back inside."

The dinner was still rolling along in fine fashion when they returned. Canary was wedged in between Natasha and Devon, the latter of whom had insisted he sit next to her, and judging by the slightly dazed looks on their faces the old woman had yet to come up for air.

"—which is when I said, 'Lydia, you know what you have. And running around chasing after every stray Tom, Dick, and Harold in Poughkeepsie isn't going to change a flippin' thing.'"

Gabriel and Julian paused in the doorframe, but the others were nodding quite seriously.

"That's sound advice," Natasha said sagely.

"It certainly is," Devon seconded quickly. "But let me ask you this." He swiveled around in his chair, staring at Canary like she possessed the nuclear launch codes. "What exactly did you mean...*drowned in a puddle*?"

Gabriel sank back into his chair with a soft groan as his friend's instant devotion to the strange woman suddenly made sense. Another bottle of wine, and his ego would never recover. "Dev, do you think that maybe you should do a patrol around the neighborhood?" he interjected swiftly. "Stop asking after *things that don't concern you—*"

"Actually, I think it's high time you boys tell us what the plan is." Canary set her napkin down on her empty plate with sudden finality. "Assuming there is, in fact, a plan."

A sudden silence fell over the room as the men sitting in front of her squirmed like errant school boys. Old women had a way of doing that to younger men. Of holding them accountable.

"I know a tracker in England who's working on finding Stryder's new location," Gabriel replied quietly. "He's been moving around a lot, but as soon as he settles he'll tell us where."

Canary nodded slowly, her bright eyes darting from face to face. "And then what?"

There was another awkward pause as the men shared a silent look.

"And then we'll take care of it."

He said it simply.

Borderline casually.

When it was anything but. The first time he'd tried to 'take care of Stryder,' the man had emptied a gun into his chest. As it stood, he had no better idea as to how to attack. If the man was immune to ink, it didn't matter how many people Gabriel brought with him. They would still be fighting with their strongest hand tied behind their backs.

"You'll *take care of it*," Canary repeated caustically. It appeared that she, too, recalled something of his previous attempt. "Like you took care of it before? When you almost bled out on the carpet, woke up in Brooklyn, and swore a divine oath of allegiance to Magda's fish?"

Devon set down his fork, looking like Christmas had come early. "Okay, hang on a second. He swore a divine oath of allegiance to—"

"Drop it." Gabriel's voice was light, but it was clear the dinner party had come to an end. The cheerful atmosphere had vanished the second he said the fateful word. Stryder. "Why don't you guys head into the living room?" he suggested casually, pushing to his feet with a tight smile. "Jules and I can clean this up."

STARING AT THE FUTURE

"Don't be silly." Canary beat him to it, taking the stack of plates out of his hand. "You go be with Natasha. I'd like to spend some time with Julian anyway."

Devon hid a quick smile as Julian glanced up, looking pale. "You would?"

"Of course I would, young man!" She pulled him to his feet, rewarding his mild panic with a swarthy grin. "It isn't every day you get to meet a world-class psychic." She handed off the plates and watched as he vanished into the kitchen. "Especially one as handsome as you..."

By now, both Gabriel and Devon were having a hard time keeping it together. But Natasha was stern. "Canary, you leave him alone. He's a sweet guy who's done nothing to deserve you."

"Oh, keep your hair on!" Canary smoothed her skirt, reaching into her purse to apply a dab of lipstick. "I may be older than the pyramids but I can still *look*, can't I?"

Devon squeezed her shoulder with a grin as he headed to the living room, the others fast on his heels. "Knock yourself out."

Despite whatever tragic hilarity might have been happening in the kitchen, the others actually had a rather fine time. Safe in their penthouse suite, reunited with their lost member, it was easy to forget what had sent them there in the first place. It was easy to compartmentalize the horror and live in the moment. If only for a little while.

They talked for the better part of an hour, pausing with occasional grins as they heard random bouts of laughter coming from the kitchen. Deliberately avoiding any mention of Stryder and 'the plan,' Devon promptly suggested that Natasha come and visit them all in London.

"My wife would love to meet you." His face softened with the same tenderness it did whenever he thought about Rae. "So would my daughter. So would Gabriel's sister, in fact."

"Is that true?" Natasha turned with a bit of trepidation to Gabriel. She had seen enough of Angel in his mind to know that she wasn't exactly the easiest person in the world. Nor, for that matter, would she be particularly inclined to welcome her older brother's new girlfriend. "Don't you think she'd just freeze me somewhere and leave me for dead?"

"There's always a chance," Gabriel said lightly, shifting slightly so that she tilted back into his arms. "But the two of you actually have a lot in common. More than Molly or Rae."

There was a sudden crash in the kitchen, and the three of them glanced over at the same time. He and Devon did a silent rock-paper-scissors, after which Gabriel pushed to his feet to go see what the trouble was. And quite possibly defend his future brother-in-law's honor...

"I don't understand."

The second he heard Julian's voice, his smile faded. A wave of tension coursed through his body and he froze where he stood, peering silently around the corner into the kitchen.

Julian and Canary were standing in front of the sink. Judging by the half-empty bottle of wine, they'd clearly been having a delightful conversation, but all that was finished now. Julian's face was pale, and he was leaning slightly off-balance against the counter, the same way he did when he had a sudden vision that caught him off-guard.

"You can't do that to him." A quiet sense of urgency strained the edges of his voice as he stared down into her eyes. "Eliza, *please*. We have a healer who can—"

"Julian Decker, I am almost nine hundred years old." Her eyes crinkled with a sage smile at the look of young indignation in front of her. "I've served my time. It's time that I move on."

She spoke with a calm self-assuredness, but Julian refused to back down. In fact, Gabriel had rarely seen him so fired up.

"Then why did you do it? Why did you let him get so close?" His eyes flashed angrily, but there was something else there as well. A deep sadness. One that had no cure. "That isn't easy for him, you know—"

"What's going on in here?"

The two looked up with a start to see Gabriel leaning in the doorway. A faint smile was fixed on his face, but his eyes were sharp as he looked at each of them in turn.

Julian flushed and looked away, but Canary gave him a huge smile.

She set down the rag she'd been using to dry the dishes and crossed over to him, linking her arm through his own. "We were just talking about you, my dear. Come on, let's take a walk..."

The moon was out and the air was freezing cold by the time the two of them hit the sidewalk outside the hotel. Twice, Gabriel offered her his jacket. In the

STARING AT THE FUTURE

131

end, he ended up simply draping it over her stubborn shoulders as they picked a random direction and started wandering slowly up the street.

"You know," she began with no provocation, "I really thought that journal of yours would be your undoing. I see now that I was wrong. It's your very salvation, Gabriel."

"What were you and Julian talking about?" he asked sharply, refusing to be deterred. "I know that expression. What did he see?"

"Facing those demons in your past, demanding answers. You've come farther than—"

"What did Julian see?"

There was a little pause, then she glanced down with a sigh. "Well, I didn't ask him directly, but I suppose he saw the fact that I have end-stage cancer and have refused treatment."

Why did you do it? Why did you let him get so close?

Gabriel's face paled as he looked down at her in horror. End-stage...? Then what was this? Some final project? He was her last wayward soul?

"It may seem selfish," she continued gently, "it certainly seemed that way to Julian, but I won't make any apologies. There's something special about you, Gabriel. I couldn't stay away."

"You have..." Gabriel trailed off in shock, unable to wrap his mind around it. He didn't give a damn how it seemed, he cared about what it was. "You have cancer and you're refusing treatment? You're dying?" He was unable to keep his voice steady. It kept shaking, either from anger or simply from fear. When he asked the final question, however, it was hard and flat. "Why?"

She took one look at his furious, heartbroken face and burst out laughing. He pulled away with a glare when she reached for him but she latched on anyway, yanking his head down to give him a noisy kiss on the cheek. "Because I'm done, Gabriel. I'm just...*done*."

A completely unacceptable answer. One he had no intention of respecting.

"Well, you may be *done*, but I'm certainly not finished with you," he replied coldly. "I'm not going to let you die, you old crone. You're going to outlive us all."

She cackled again, looking at him with great affection. "Well, if this Stryder fellow has anything to do with it, that might actually be true. But if it isn't..." Her eyes misted over as she reached up once again to touch his face. "Just know that nothing in the world has made me happier than watching how you've changed since you got to Brooklyn. The man standing before me now is not the same man who jogged past my apartment that night. You've found yourself, Gabriel. You've changed. And I...I really couldn't be prouder."

"Then don't leave," he said quietly. "Jules is right. We have a healer. This doesn't have to be a goodbye. Come back with us to London, and—"

"Gabriel," she admonished gently, her eyes twinkling in the light of the waning moon, "I'm tired. Tired, and happy, and peaceful...and done. It's time for me to rest."

There was a charged silence, after which she chuckled again.

"But you're not going to accept that, are you?"

He shook his head defiantly, not surrendering an inch. "If anything's going to kill you, it's going to be me. I earned that right weeks ago. You're not taking it away from me."

She laughed again, long and loud, before steering them back in the direction of the hotel. "Just promise me something, will you?" Her hand gripped his sleeve, pulling him to a sudden stop. "Promise me that you'll finish this quest, Gabriel. Not the one with Stryder, but the one with the book. It's the only way you'll find peace. It's the only way you'll move on."

A soft smile settled in her eyes, one Gabriel knew he'd remember forever.

"It's the only way you'll get the future we both know you deserve."

WHEN GABRIEL AND CANARY got back to the penthouse that evening she went straight to sleep, pausing only to demand she get the biggest bed and to throw a suggestive wink at Julian.

Gabriel wandered into the living room in a daze, his head spinning with everything he'd just heard, hardly aware of the intoxicated conversation going on around him.

"So...*everything*," Natasha was saying, shaking her head in disbelief and looking at Julian like he was some sort of god. "You can basically see *everything*."

"Not everything," he answered quickly, too modest for his own good. "The psychic connection is pretty new. I'm still trying to work it out."

STARING AT THE FUTURE

"But that's *incredible*!" she insisted, leaning back against the couch with a beaming smile. "Your dad has to be so proud."

Julian froze for a second as Devon slowly looked up from his glass of wine. The whole thing only lasted a moment, but it was enough to make Natasha stop in her tracks.

"I mean...unless you got the tatù from your mom?"

She glanced at Gabriel for help, then quickly realized that they had bigger problems.

"Hey, what's the matter?" She pushed to her feet and came to his side, staring up at his face in concern. Over her shoulder, Julian met his eyes for the briefest moment. Offering silent understanding. Silent support. "Did something—"

"Come to bed?"

It was a quiet request, and one that she immediately accepted. After bidding the others a quick goodnight, the two of them disappeared into their bedroom. Alone at last.

"What happened?" she asked again, standing frozen beside the mattress as Gabriel slowly took off his shoes. "And don't say 'nothing': Canary was right about you being a terrible liar."

"Did you know she has end-stage cancer?"

He was going to phrase it more delicately. Ease into it with a gentle transition. But looking up at Natasha's face, he was suddenly certain that she already knew.

Sure enough, a wave of sadness crashed down on her. Followed by a quiet sigh. "Yeah, I did. She was diagnosed a few months ago. Her sick days..." She trailed off, staring down miserably at the bed. "That's when I started bringing her food."

Gabriel took a second to absorb this, catching on faster than most, before quietly shaking his head. "Why didn't you tell me? Why didn't *she* tell me?"

Natasha came to sit beside him, putting a gentle hand on his shoulder. "There was no point in you knowing. She wanted to fix you and send you on your way. She didn't want you to get hit with one final trauma before you left. She wanted you happy. We...we both do."

He cast her a sideways glance, lifting his arm with a sigh, leaning them both back against the headboard as she nestled underneath. "It just seems so..."

"I know it does," she interrupted gently, "but you have to consider her age. She's lived a long life, Gabriel. She's happy with it, and most everyone she knows is dead. She's ready to go."

Well, maybe I'm not ready to let her go.

He wanted desperately to say it. Tried to think of a million different ways to do so, but couldn't come up with anything that didn't make him sound like a petulant child. In the end he merely settled down on the bed beside her, closing his eyes as the long day came to a close.

"Did I say something to offend Julian?" He felt her body stiffen, and glanced down in concern. "Earlier, when I mentioned his parents... I really didn't mean to—"

"Not at all," Gabriel said swiftly. "Jules got the ink from his dad, but Jacob isn't really in the picture anymore." He hesitated, then glanced at her again. "You saw him. In my mind."

"I saw Julian's dad?" Her face screwed up with a frown before clearing with sudden horror. "*Jacob*? The guy in the cell? The one who was brainwashed and now—"

"That's him."

She fell silent for a moment, reeling from the heartbreaking image, then she squinted her eyes shut and banged her head against the wall. "Way to go, Stone. Brilliant first impression. Bring up the guy's absentee father—"

She might have said more, but Gabriel didn't hear it. He was having trouble hearing anything past that first phrase. His entire body came alive as he sat up in bed, staring down at her with a sudden realization. "Stone. Your last name is Stone."

She paused her self-defamation long enough to give him a strained look. "Gabriel, we've slept together. Please tell me you didn't forget my last name."

"No, I didn't forget, I just... I just didn't put it together." Without another word he sprang out of bed, rifling around in his bag until he came up with a worn leather journal. "Stone. As in Benjamin Stone. A mnemokinetic who worked for Jonathon Cromfield."

"Let me see that." She snatched it out of his hands, eyes flickering down at the entry on the page. She read for a moment, then closed it slowly. "Well, I know he shouldn't have been working for Cromfield, but it sounds like the guy

STARING AT THE FUTURE

prevented war with Spain. So maybe, karmically speaking, these things sort of cancel out?"

"No. I don't care about that." Gabriel took back the book and opened it to the same page. "It says that Benjamin has the ability to retrieve *or destroy* memories. He could do both."

Natasha paused for a moment, looking at him very carefully. "And you're asking if I can do the same?"

Gabriel didn't answer right away. He fell silent, his head swirling with a hundred possibilities he had never considered before. The possibility of a fresh start. The kind he couldn't get from merely working through his problems. The kind that came from being wiped clean.

"When I was seventeen, I got hit with a piece of shrapnel in Bermuda. It collapsed one of my lungs and I lay there on the sand for nine hours, gasping for breath, waiting for one of two things to happen. For someone to find me, or for me to die."

He spoke in a quiet monotone. Not a bit of inflection in his voice.

"The day I turned twenty, Cromfield handed me a grenade launcher and told me to blow a hole in the House of Lords. A test. When I refused, he had me stripped naked and beaten to within an inch of my life."

Natasha trembled, but he wasn't trying to scare her. Quite the contrary. He leaned towards her, gently squeezing her hand.

"I break out in a cold sweat every time I hear a car backfire. I speak twelve different languages, but I learned them so I could travel the world and kill. Even after all our work, I still have no idea whether I have a middle name, and I swear to you, Natasha, until the day I die I'm going to sleep within reach of a gun."

He fell silent, pulling in shallow breaths as he stared deep into her eyes.

"I shouldn't know how to do all those things. I shouldn't..." He broke off suddenly, making up his mind. "I don't want to."

Natasha saw where he was going and quickly leaned back, shaking her head in advance as if to ward off the question. "Just wait a second, okay? Don't ask me—"

"Take them away." He sat right in front of her, forcing her to look him in the eyes. "My memories. Take them away. I don't want them anymore."

"Absolutely not."

"Natasha, I want this. I'm sure."

"But you shouldn't want it, Gabriel!" she exclaimed, pulling away from him. "You shouldn't be sure! You think I don't want to go back and erase the memory of my parents' car crash? It's as painful as it is *fundamentally* necessary. It makes us who we are!"

"But I don't want to be this person," he answered quietly. "I didn't have a choice, but if I had I wouldn't have chosen this." His eyes burned bright in the dim light as they locked onto hers. "Take away Stryder, and I won't fight him. Take away my father, and I...I won't be plagued by these questions. Don't you see? If you take this part of me away, then it can't hurt us anymore. We can start fresh, move on. I won't be responsible for dragging you into my—"

"And what about Jacob?" she demanded, throwing up her hands. "We were *just* talking about him. You think Jacob's glad to not have his memories?! You think he wouldn't give anything he had just to get them back? You think Julian wouldn't kill for that?!"

"It isn't the same thing—"

"Enough!" In an act of rage she threw the journal against the wall, breaking the spine before it fluttered to the floor. "This may be what you want, but it's just *wrong*! You are too strong a person to be beaten by something like this, and I'm not going to let you lessen yourself just to make things easier or safe! Especially not when—"

She broke off suddenly, freezing dead still on the bed. For a split second, their eyes locked. Then she squared her shoulders, and pulled in a deep breath.

"—especially not when I'm in love with you."

You could have heard a pin drop. The entire room was suddenly very still.

She said... She said that she's...

Gabriel didn't move. Didn't blink. Didn't even breathe. The number of women who'd implied as much over the years was endless, but none of them had really meant it. In fact, he didn't know if anyone had ever said those words to him before now.

She's in love with me.

But even more surprising than her confession was his sudden reaction. The words that seemed to come out of nowhere spilling awkwardly into the room.

"I love you, too."

STARING AT THE FUTURE

137

A smile so bright it seemed to light up the entire room danced across her face. Her teeth clamped down on her lower lip, and for a second he thought she was going to forget the argument entirely and throw her arms around his neck.

But she didn't. The smile was forced back into hiding as she proceeded calmly.

"Good. Well, in that case, you should know my conditions."

Gabriel's eyebrows shot into his hair, and he laughed in spite of himself. The room itself seemed to be laughing with him. Like he'd had one too many drinks. "You have conditions?"

"I do indeed." Another radiant smile flashed across her face, but she grew abruptly serious. "Your past, your present, your future—I want all of it. I want *you*, Gabriel Alden. I love you. And you need to do this. Whether you want to or not."

His own smile faded as he realized she was right. Now was no time for shortcuts or quick fixes. Every single person in his life had been waiting for him to turn the page. A little shiver ran up his arms as she settled on the bed in front of him. That age-old question in her eyes.

"No secrets?"

He hesitated a second longer, then nodded his head.

"No secrets."

Then he took her hands and the two of them dove into the past. One last time.

Chapter 13

IT WAS SUNNY. THAT was the one thing that stood out sharper than anything else in Gabriel's mind. It had been a perfect, sunny day. The day his world came to an end.

He and Natasha descended through the bright sky, planting their feet on the soft grass as they lifted their heads to look around them. The sights and smells of the city were gone, and all at once they were in a woodland paradise. A sea of sunlit green stretching as far as the eye could see.

This is where you grew up? Natasha's voice echoed in his mind, breathless with wonder as she stared around at the emerald hills. *This is your home?*

It wasn't where he grew up. It was supposed to be, but he had very few memories of the place. Nevertheless, his head turned automatically as a whispered breeze echoed through the copse of trees. His eyes danced with reflected light as he gazed down the hill at the lake below.

Yeah...this was my home.

"Gabriel!"

A sudden voice called out from across the lawn, and he turned his head towards the house. His tan skin went very pale, and every muscle seemed to lock down as a man walked through the front door into the yard. A man who looked very much like Gabriel himself.

"Gabriel! I called you in for lunch twenty minutes ago!"

There was a blur of golden hair as a tiny child streaked across the grass. His father might have been yelling for him, but the boy was in no way afraid. In fact, he picked up speed with a mischievous grin and launched himself through the air, landing right in his father's arms.

"Oh, you think this is funny, do you?!"

Gabriel's heart tightened with some long-forgotten emotion as he watched them laughing together in the sun. Tightened to the point of physical pain as he tried to pull in a breath.

STARING AT THE FUTURE

"Were you down by the lake again?" Michael Alden stopped tickling his son just long enough to let him catch his breath. "Find anything good?"

Young Gabriel's beaming face grew abruptly serious. "I think I saw a dolphin."

"A dolphin!" Michael threw back his head with a sparkling laugh. A laugh that sounded identical to his adult son's. "Well, that deserves a little investigation..."

He trailed off at the sound of crunching gravel, shielding his eyes against the sun as a black car with tinted windows rolled towards them over the long drive. For a split-second, a flicker of fear shadowed across his handsome face. But the next moment, he was smiling once more.

"Hey, buddy, do me a favor." He set Gabriel down, angling him towards the house. "Go inside and get cleaned up for lunch. Wait for me in your room, okay? Wait right there."

"Okay!"

Gabriel was off like a shot, darting inside the house with a carefree grin. He didn't see the car park around the corner of the house. Or the man who stepped onto the drive. He didn't see the way his father stood in front of the door, folding his arms threateningly across his chest.

"Aaron," he greeted the man curtly.

"Michael."

By now, Gabriel was at the end of his rope. He leaned forward in his shoes, desperate to hear every word. But there was a sudden tug deep in his abdomen, and before he knew what was happening he felt himself floating into the air once more.

Wait—what's going on?! He whirled around in a panic, trying to see through the sudden fog. *Natasha, bring us back!*

That isn't your memory, she answered apologetically. *You weren't there yourself.*

She couldn't bring them back, but she did the next best thing. Just a second later, they were standing inside a child's bedroom. A bedroom that had been transformed into a virtual shrine for King Arthur and his knights. Taped to the walls were a hundred hand-drawn pictures of Camelot, and littered across the floor were a slew of plastic swords.

I don't remember any of this... Gabriel made a slow rotation around the four corners, completely ignoring his three-year-old self. *This must have been after he took me to Hadrian's—*

"—can't believe you came here," a deep voice snapped from the other room. "This is my *home*, Aaron. This is where I live with my son. You have no business—"

"Ah, but Mr. Cromfield seems to think that it is his business. In fact, I hear that he's very curious to meet your son."

At this point little Gabriel abandoned his search for a sweater, and crept noiselessly down the hall. The older Gabriel and Natasha followed along, keeping perfectly quiet and sticking to the shadows even though they were at no risk of being either seen or heard.

"I gave Cromfield twenty years. *Twenty* years." Michael's voice burned with the deepest loathing as he stared the man down. "He's taken enough. This is my life now."

An unexpected look of sympathy flashed across Stryder's face, but it was replaced almost immediately with a sick smile. "I'm afraid he disagrees."

"Fine," Michael growled, moving across the room to grab his keys off the wall. "Then I'll go and speak with him myself—"

"That won't be necessary," Stryder interrupted quietly. "He's made it clear that he has no further wish to speak with you."

Michael paused mid-step, hand still reaching for the wall. For a moment, he simply looked surprised. Then an expression of chilled understanding spread across his face. "Are you here to kill me, Aaron?"

Such a terrifying question, asked in such a quiet voice. Young Gabriel sucked in a quiet gasp and watched with wide eyes as the man talking to his father pulled out a gun.

"I'm sorry, Michael." Stryder clicked the safety off the weapon, pointing it straight at his friend's chest. "This wasn't what I wanted. I think you know that."

"You're acting like you don't have a choice. But you do." Michael lifted his hands with exaggerated slowness. "I don't want to hurt you either, Aaron."

Only someone with the same tatù could tell that the move was in no way placating. He was using his ink. Trying to get some sort of hold on Stryder.

But it was an effort that was doomed to fail.

STARING AT THE FUTURE

141

"You think I don't know what you're doing?" Stryder asked with a wry smile. "That I haven't seen you do the same thing a thousand times before? You're a legend, Michael."

For the first time, Michael took a small step back. Placing his body in between Stryder and the hall that led to his son's room. There was an ashen tint to his skin, and a faint tremor in his hands that hadn't been there before.

"Aaron...my son." A note of panic tightened the edges of his voice as he inched closer to the hall. "He's innocent in all this—"

"Not for long." Stryder leveled the weapon with a small sigh. "I told you, Cromfield's very interested in meeting the boy. Apparently, he'll take one Alden in place of another."

"I'll go back," Michael said immediately, his eyes locked on the gun.

By now, he had surely realized there was no moving it. Any more than he could secure a deadly grip on Stryder's blood. Any more than he could bury the kitchen knives in the man's chest. He was both directly and indirectly immune. The perfect weapon. "Aaron, let me go back and talk to him. You know how he gets. He's just angry." He was standing in front of the hallway now. White as a sheet. "Let me try to reason with him—"

"Reason with Cromfield?" The gun lowered a few inches, and Stryder let out a quiet laugh. "Michael, you know better than that. He's made up his mind. About you, and about Gabriel. I'm sorry, I truly am."

The sound of his son's name propelled Michael into action. His eyes flashed with the fiercest rage and he took a step forward—only to immediately fall back again as the gun was leveled once more at his chest. As Stryder's finger wrapped around the trigger he slowly lowered his hands back to his sides, staring with a quiet sort of dread across the kitchen.

"We can leave," he murmured. "Let us leave and you'll never hear from us again. Say the child was gone when you got here. Cromfield will think we're both dead."

Stryder shook his head with a sad smile. "Until someone in his endless network of spies tells him you're alive, and then he kills me for lying."

"Aaron—"

"Michael, I'm sorry."

The man's finger tightened, but a second before he could pull the trigger there was a tiny cry as Gabriel flew out of the shadows, standing in front of his father with open arms.

"GABRIEL—*NO!*"

The gun came down immediately as Michael snatched his son into the air, turning so his tiny body was shielded from potential harm. After a quick check to make sure he was all right he pressed a fierce kiss to his son's forehead, his eyes spilling over with tears. "Gabriel, run outside. Run outside and keep running until you can't run anymore."

Stryder raised the gun again with a touch of impatience, standing in between the child and the door. "Don't make this more difficult—"

"He cannot have him."

A shot rang out. Sufficiently ending everything that happened before it. Forever changing everything that would happen after. There was a piercing scream as both Gabriels cried out in horror, then watched in total silence as their father's body fell to the floor.

The world around them seemed to dim, as if the sun itself had covered its eyes. Stryder stood there for a moment, staring at the crimson puddle on the floor before he briskly strode across the room and lifted Gabriel into his arms. "Come on, kid. Everybody's waiting for you."

The memory dimmed, and Gabriel came back to the present in tears. It was like that first time Natasha had taken him into the past, when he was unable to fully come out of it. He simply sat there on the mattress, arms wrapped around his stomach as he silently gasped for breath.

"Oh, sweetheart..."

Natasha came up behind him, wrapping her slender arms around his own. She rested her forehead against the back of his neck and waited there until slowly, ever so slowly, the shock subsided enough that he was able to speak.

"He didn't give me away," he said in a daze. "He wanted me to run. He wanted to keep me away from it—"

"Of course he did." Natasha circled around to the front and swept back his hair. There were tears in her eyes, but had yet to fall. "You thought it was his choice?"

"I didn't know," Gabriel murmured, his eyes fixing on nothing in particular as the images played back in his head. "I didn't understand how he could hate

STARING AT THE FUTURE

me so much that he would trade my life for his own. I didn't understand what I must have done—"

His voice cut off, choked with emotion, and Natasha grabbed him in a tight embrace. He buried his face in her hair, letting it wash over him like the waves of a choppy sea.

It didn't matter what he'd thought before: he'd been wrong. Stryder had lied to him, and he had been wrong. It wasn't a question of something he'd done, some terrible slight that had made him somehow unworthy of his father's love. All Michael Alden ever wanted to do was protect him. To keep him safe from the shadows the chased them. He gave his very life for it.

Strange as it was, horrific as those images were, Gabriel's lips curled up into the most unlikely of smiles. It was as though a weight had finally lifted. One he'd been carrying his entire life. One he'd gotten so used to, now that it was gone he felt as though he could fly away.

But such moments are few and far between. And never meant to last long.

There was a sudden knock on the door, and the couple pulled apart. Gabriel took a second to get himself under control before calling, "Yeah, what is it?"

"It's Stryder," Devon called back, tense with anticipation. "We found him."

Stryder.

The man's face swam fresh in Gabriel's mind. The ingrained cruelty. The sad, ineffectual smile. A wave of hatred unlike anything he'd ever felt coursed hot through his veins, and he found himself pushing to his feet without making the conscious decision to do so.

"Let me get my coat."

"Gabriel, wait a second." Natasha leapt to her feet as Devon moved away, assumedly to make preparations to leave. "You know what I said before? I take it all back. You were right, okay? You forget Stryder, then you don't fight him. Let's just forget him together right now."

Gabriel caught her hands with a smile as she reached for his face, kissing them tenderly before lowering them back to her sides. "I thought you wanted me. All of me."

She shook her head quickly, the image of the gun dancing fearfully in her eyes. "I changed my mind. We could streamline you a little. That would still be fine. I'd settle."

"I wouldn't."

The words surprised him as much as they did her. Arrogance and self-esteem had been instinctually conflated in his time spent with Cromfield. One rising to prominence to cover the acute absence of the other. But things had changed now. Things were no longer his fault.

With a steadiness that surprised him, he leaned down for a gentle kiss.

"I'll be back before sunrise. I promise."

She nodded shakily, folding her arms protectively across her chest as she shrank back onto the bed. He gathered his things quickly and had almost made it to the door, when she called out suddenly, almost as if she was afraid he'd walk away and never hear. "Gabriel...I really do love you."

He paused where he stood, his face lighting up with a secret smile. He might be on the verge of walking into the world's greatest darkness, but for the first time in his life he felt as though he could stop dwelling on the past. Stop living moment to moment. And maybe, just maybe, he could do the unthinkable.

He could start looking to the future.

"I love you, too."

"WHY DO BAD GUYS ALWAYS hide in warehouses?" Devon muttered, gazing up at the darkened building with a comically over-simplified view. "We don't hide in warehouses."

"Well, we're not...how did you put it?" Julian flashed him a grin. "Bad guys."

"We are tonight." Gabriel stepped forward to stand in between them, hands in his pockets as his gaze fixed firmly on the door. "We take no prisoners in there. This thing ends tonight." He glanced to his right and left, staring at each friend in turn. "Agreed?"

"Agreed," Devon answered automatically.

Julian paused a moment before nodding his consent. "Agreed."

"Just remember," Gabriel continued in a low voice, "while Stryder's ink will affect you, yours won't be able to affect him. It's like when Mallins stabbed Rae. Because he was the one wielding the blade, she couldn't heal. It's why I couldn't mess with his gun; he was holding it."

STARING AT THE FUTURE

Devon nodded seriously, fixing his eyes on the prize. But as the three of them started to take a step forward, Julian's hand flashed out suddenly and pulled Gabriel back.

"You're coming home after this, right?" he asked anxiously. "Back to London?"

Gabriel glanced back in surprise, gently tugging his sleeve free. "Uh...yeah. At some point in the near future. This really isn't the time to discuss—"

"You need to come home," Julian said abruptly. He faltered a second under Gabriel's piercing stare, and his shoulders fell with a soft sigh. "Angel's pregnant."

The words hit like a battering ram, straight to the heart.

"I didn't want you to find out like this," he continued softly. "I'm sure she wanted to do it herself, but it's been *months* that you've been away, and she needs you—"

"Angie's pregnant." Gabriel repeated the words , testing them out while he tried to convince himself. A wave of unexpected emotion welled up in his chest, and he found himself shaking his head with a wondrous smile. "Of course she is. She's been trying to tell me..."

He thought back to all the missed calls. All the angry voice messages. All the midnight text messages asking when he was coming home. The last time he'd been in London, he'd promised to see her. Then the journal happened, and he'd never showed.

He thought about it for a second more, trying to wrap his head around the idea of a tiny little niece or nephew, then he let out a bark of laughter and caught Julian in a sudden embrace.

"Congratulations!"

Julian tensed up for a second, like he wasn't sure if Gabriel was going to hug him or hit him, before relaxing in sudden exhaustion. "Thanks. You're right, though, it's hardly the time—"

"No, Jules. You absolutely can't go in there."

Julian pulled back in surprise, glancing once at the warehouse before returning to Gabriel with a hint of confusion. "What are you talking about? We're right here—"

"And you think I'm going to risk my niece or nephew growing up without a father?" Gabriel shook his head, standing firmly in the way. "Not a bloody chance."

"Come on, man, don't be ridiculous. Devon's out here, and he has a kid."

But Devon seemed to wholeheartedly agree. The second Gabriel took a stand, he instantly joined him. Blocking the door with the same uncompromising smile.

"Go back to the apartment and book us on the next flight to London. And call Angel while you're at it. Let her know you're coming home so she won't stress."

"I can't believe this!" Julian stepped back in shock. "We're standing *right* outside the building. Let's just go inside, and—"

"*No.*"

The men said it at the same time, shoving him back towards the street. While Devon flashed him a wicked grin, Gabriel raised his hand and hailed down a cab. He gave the driver the address before forcibly putting Julian inside.

"You need to get back to my sister. And let her know I'll be right behind you."

The door slammed shut before the psychic could say anything, and Gabriel tossed a handful of bills up to the front. It was just pulling away from the curb, when it paused and the window rolled down.

"Gabriel, you said your niece or nephew? Well...it's a niece." Julian's face lit up with an indescribable glow. "We're having a girl."

A girl.

Gabriel pulled in a deep breath, vaguely aware that his fingers had started trembling. He stuffed them quickly into his pockets as his lips curved up into a radiant smile. "Don't have her without me."

Julian flashed a final smile as the cab pulled away into the dark. Taking him back to the apartment in Manhattan. Taking him one step closer to home.

"You ready to do this?" Devon clapped Gabriel on the back, looking him up and down with a faint grin. "In case you failed to remember I, too, have a child waiting at home."

Gabriel flipped up his collar against the wind. "Yeah, but yours would be better off without you."

STARING AT THE FUTURE   147

Devon grinned as he made his way towards the warehouse door. "You're going to make a terrible uncle."

They kicked it down at the same time. Sending it flying back fifty feet to land on the floor with a hollow clatter. The second it settled they walked cautiously into the building, taking in every detail at a glance with their hands at the ready.

"It looks empty," Devon murmured, his keen senses picking up on nothing but old furniture and a broken- down refrigerator. "Are you sure Kraigan texted the right—"

A screaming siren suddenly echoed off the walls. Growing louder and louder with every piercing pass. Vibrating at a pitch that rattled the dusty windows in their frames.

Gabriel flinched, while Devon clapped his hands over his ears and bowed his head with a soft gasp. When the siren grew impossibly louder he actually knelt to the floor, throwing out a hand for balance as his eyes squinted shut against the noise.

It was only then that Gabriel realized his friend's ears were bleeding.

"Devon!" he shouted in alarm.

But for the very first time, Devon couldn't hear him. The vibrations were wreaking havoc on his heightened senses, torturing him with a pain so incapacitating he was unable to move.

Without a second thought Gabriel grabbed him by the arm and dragged him back out of the building, setting him gently on the sidewalk as a stream of blood poured down both sides of his neck. The second they were over the threshold the siren suddenly stopped, leaving a surreal silence in its wake.

A silence that came with a clear message.

"It has to be me," Gabriel panted, placing a steadying hand on Devon's back. "Just me."

Devon tried to answer, but the second he moved his jaw he was hit with another wave of excruciating pain. His eardrums had burst. There was no going back now. Another few seconds in that room, and he'd be deaf forever.

Still, Devon Wardell wasn't known to go down without a fight.

"Just give me a second," he gasped, gritting his teeth against the pain. "I'm not letting you go in there by yourself. Give me a second, and we'll figure something out—"

"*Hey.*" Gabriel knelt in front of him, wincing sympathetically before squeezing his shoulder with a reassuring smile. "This was always my fight. It was always going to be me."

Devon stared at him for a minute, then shook his head. A second later he pushed shakily to his feet, swaying slightly as he struggled to find his balance. "Not a chance. We're both—"

But Gabriel had already hailed down another cab.

For the second time in less than five minutes, he shoved a reluctant friend down onto the leather seat and told the driver where to go. After tossing up another handful of cash, and warning the driver his passenger might not be able to hear him for a while, he took a step back and tapped twice on the hood, sending the last of his reinforcements on his way.

As the cab disappeared into the darkness he turned around, staring at the broken door.

"You wanted me? I'm right here."

A man walked out of the shadows as Gabriel walked into them. The same man he'd seen shoot his father less than an hour before. An almost feral hatred surged through him but he kept it carefully off his face, walking steadily to the middle of the floor.

The two men stared at each other for a moment before Stryder took a small step back.

"You know, the strangest thing keeps happening to me. My people keep turning up at various locations all over the city. Bound, bleeding, arrested." He tilted his head with an indulgent smile. "You wouldn't happen to know anything about that, would you?"

Gabriel forced a smile in return. "Well, when you misplace your toys other people are bound to play with them."

Stryder laughed, folding his hands behind his back. "Well said. Too true." The laughter faded as Stryder studied him intently, struck with a sudden feeling of déjà vu. "So how are we doing this tonight? We going to battle it out?"

Gabriel regarded him calmly. "I have people waiting for me at home. I'd rather just get it over with, if you don't mind."

"As you wish."

STARING AT THE FUTURE   149

Without a second's pause, Stryder pulled a handgun out of the waistband of his pants. It shimmered in the darkness, catching every glint of moonlight straining in through the dirty glass.

"Well, this feels familiar." Stryder flicked off the safety with a sinister grin. "Haven't I shot you once before? Or maybe that was Michael. The two of you look so much alike..."

Gabriel didn't move a muscle. He could tell Stryder was still talking, still callously taunting him, but his eyes were locked on the target. Locked on the gun.

A bullet travelling at seventeen hundred miles per hour, needed only .25 seconds to reach a target standing fifty feet away. Gabriel was standing quite a bit closer than that. Nearer to twenty.

"...wasn't his biggest mistake. His biggest mistake was..."

By his estimations, he would have a little less than .1 seconds to act. A feat that even Cromfield had never attempted. A feat that promised almost certain death.

"...begged for his life, you know."

Gabriel tuned back in to the conversation to see Stryder staring up at him with a sneer.

"Your father begged like a dog. Offered me your life instead."

The world went suddenly quiet as everything sharpened into sudden focus.

"My father did beg," Gabriel answered quietly, but with something else in his voice. Steel maybe? "But he begged for my life. He did everything in his power to keep me away from you. It's a battle that ends tonight."

The sneer melted off Stryder's face, replaced instead with a cold smile. "You think you're faster than a bullet, kid? That's the one lesson your father never learned."

Gabriel's lips twitched up in a wry grin. "I'm not my father."

He sensed the bullet before he heard it. Felt the warm vibrations as they rippled through the air. His hands were still in his pockets, but he knew at once he wouldn't need them. He didn't need anything other than exactly what was inside him. In the end, he closed his eyes.

There was a whisper of air as the bullet changed direction mid-flight. A choking scream erupted as it buried itself in Stryder's chest. For a second the man just stood there, stunned. Then a fountain of blood blossomed over his shirt. His head dropped down to stare at his chest as blood began to run out of his mouth. He crumpled to the ground.

Dead.

A sigh of the deepest relief rushed out of Gabriel as he slowly opened his eyes. They focused for a split-second on the body in front of him. The corpse of the man who had murdered his father. All his life had led to this moment. He realized it now. Like looking in a mirror, trying to see the past. Then Gabriel turned back to the horizon, never to think of him again.

It was over.

It was time to go home.

GABRIEL HAD A KEY, but he still crawled in through the second-story window. The glass eased up silently and dropped down behind him without a sound. No one in the bedroom was the wiser. They were curled up like nothing had ever happened, fast asleep.

Not for long...

With a little grin, Gabriel pulled a receipt out of his pocket, rolled it up into a little ball, and tossed it strategically at the bed. It landed exactly where it was supposed to. There was a hitch in deep breathing, and Julian Decker slowly opened his eyes.

He stared blankly into the dark for a moment, trying get his bearings, before his eyes fell upon the golden-haired trespasser perched in the window. The two of them locked eyes for a split-second—one with a mischievous grin, the other blinking in heavy exhaustion—before Gabriel cocked his head towards the hallway and motioned for Julian to leave.

The psychic rolled his eyes and pulled himself out of bed, leaving brother and sister to have their long-awaited reunion in peace. It was going to be one for the books.

Gabriel waited until the sound of Julian's footsteps had faded down the hall before he climbed onto the mattress, leaning back against the headboard with a twinkling smile. "Wake up, little sister."

Angel blinked her eyes open, then stared up in shock, unable to believe it could be true. "Gabriel?" Her face brightened with pure, unadulterated joy. But

STARING AT THE FUTURE 151

just as quickly her eyes darted down to her stomach, clouding with guilt. "I wanted to tell you in person," she whispered. "I didn't think that you'd stay gone so long. And then, once I realized why you were staying away, I didn't want to be the reason you thought you had to come back—"

He pressed a soft finger over her lips, eyes glowing with a radiant smile. "I'm going to be an uncle?"

Without another word, she threw her arms around his neck and the two of them came together. In a lot of ways, it was as if he'd never left. They talked about *everything*. No matter how trivial, no matter how small. He told her about the mugging he'd stopped in Prague. She told him about how she'd accidentally frozen her first ultrasound technician. They talked about Cromfield—something the two of them *never* did. They talked about Natasha—something that Gabriel was only just starting to wrap his head around himself.

"I think Jules is going to ask me to marry him."

By now, the sun had risen over the tops of the trees. Streams of pink and gold light were flooding in through the windows, and the gauzy curtains around the window seemed to glow.

Gabriel nodded slowly, taking great care to hide the smile that was warming him from the inside out. "And what are you going to say?"

For the first time since she'd fallen asleep in his arms, all those years ago, his fearless little Angel looked a little uncertain. Her sapphire eyes darted quickly to the side, measuring his response, before she continued with caution.

"I think I'm going to say yes." Her face warmed just at the thought of it before she cast another sideways glance his way. "Unless you think I should do it with a few conditions."

Gabriel kicked off his shoes and folded his hands behind his head, his eyes twinkling with a wicked little smile. "Well, *that's* a great idea, one that requires a lot of thought..."

The two of them settled in for the long haul. Listening as Julian started rummaging around in the kitchen, making them all breakfast. Listing what they considered to be reasonable conditions for marriage, one by one.

It wasn't until they heard the dog scampering up the stairs that either one of them considered getting up for the first time. Angel slipped on a robe, while

Gabriel rudely called down their breakfast order. But before they could go down to eat, she caught him by the arm.

"This girl...Natasha." Her piercing eyes locked onto his, holding him forever accountable. "You really love her?"

A faint look of surprise danced across his face, replaced with a little smile.

A girl who makes you smile. A girl you'd do whatever it took to hold on to. The one.

"Yeah. I really do."

The adopted siblings shared a long look before Angel skipped down the stairs with a sudden grin. "You'll have to take her to the barbeque then."

Ah, yes, Rae and Devon's third wedding anniversary. A family gathering he'd long ago promised that he would attend. He just never imagined he might be bringing a date.

He paused for a second, considering, then a little smile crept over his face. "Tell them we're going to need another chair..."

Epilogue

GABRIEL STOOD ALONG the riverfront, kicking his shoes against the weathered stones. A lot had happened in the last few weeks. His mind was racing, and his eyes were lost in thought.

Julian's father had worked with Natasha and gotten his memories back. As many years as he'd been trying, they returned to him in one fell swoop. Gabriel remembered the exact moment he came out of it and opened his eyes. It was like the light came back into them. The last decade of darkness fell away, and for the first time since walking into that cell the man was alive.

Jacob took one look around the room, then made a bee-line for his son. Holding him in an embrace so strong they didn't think he would ever let go.

Julian proposed to Angel not long after.

Eliza P. Duncan had died. Gabriel had known it was coming. They both had. He remembered the morning he'd left New York, right after the showdown with Stryder. He remembered seeing her waving from the porch—knowing it would be the last time. Her work there was done. There was nothing left to do but rest.

A week later, Natasha had moved permanently to London. It was a turn of events Gabriel was still having trouble believing was real. She'd simply shown up at his old flat with a suitcase in each hand, asking if she could use his wi-fi. He'd tackled her on the landing and dragged her over the threshold, vowing never to let her leave. Even Hans was welcomed with open arms.

Two days later, she'd received an offer from the London School of Ballet.

"It's cold out here." Gabriel looked up in surprise as a tall man came to stand beside him, shoving his hands deep into the pockets of his expensive coat. "Can't we ever meet in my office?"

He turned back to the water with a faint grin. "It's good for the president to get out every now and then. Proves you're a man of the people."

Carter chuckled, then cast Gabriel a sideways glance. "I got your teleporter."

"Oh, right. Happy birthday."

"Next year, I might just prefer a card."

Gabriel bowed his head with a grin. "Duly noted."

They stood in silence for a while, each one staring out over the river. Then Carter turned to face him, looking him curiously up and down. "I was pleased you accepted my offer. The Privy Council is going to be lucky to have you. For the second time, I might add."

"Are you ever going to let me live that down—"

"The fact that you infiltrated my organization as a spy, to pass information about my stepdaughter to her worst enemy? No, Gabriel. I don't think I will."

Gabriel kicked again at the rocks, his lips curving up in a begrudging smile. "Fair enough."

Carter watched him for a moment, taking in every detail, before he cleared his throat. "So that's it, then? No more travelling? No more journal? You're back for good?"

Gabriel started nodding, then stopped himself. A faint frown shadowed across his face as he found himself blocked by the same question that had been eating away at him for months. "I still don't know who it was. I still don't know who saved me."

The past had been put to rest. The future was nothing but clear, unending horizon. But this one nagging question remained. The faceless man who had jumped in front of Gabriel at the sugar factory. The mysterious hero who'd taken the bullet in his place.

Gabriel had tried to figure it out a million times. He'd gone back in time with Natasha, but no matter what he did the face was still blurred. Like it was caught between two worlds. Out of both time and place.

"Andrew," it was the first time he'd ever used the president's first name, "for a split-second, I could have sworn it was..." He trailed off, shaking his head. There was no point in saying who he could have sworn it was, because that was utterly impossible. The man was dead. He'd died in a fire long ago. And even if he hadn't, there's no way he'd sacrifice his life to save Gabriel's.

STARING AT THE FUTURE

Carter watched him for another moment, placing a supportive hand on his shoulder. "Sometimes, we're not meant to have all the answers. Sometimes, we're meant to take things on faith. It's the only way to move forward."

Gabriel's eyes locked onto the water as he considered it. Never blinking as he stared at the churning waves. Carter stood with him for a second more before heading back to his car.

"I'll see you Monday morning, Alden. Don't be late."

Gabriel nodded quickly, his eyes still on the water. "Yes, sir."

He waited until Carter got into the car, waited until the engine revved and raced down the street, before he reached into his pocket and pulled out a worn leather book. His fingers traced the edges as his eyes flickered over the cover. For as little time as it had been in his life, he felt as though he'd been carrying it around forever.

The wind picked up and he spun it suddenly in his palm, preparing to throw it into the river, when a sudden instinct made him pull back. With an impulse he couldn't control, he opened to a random page near the end. Something he hadn't read yet.

October 12, 1993

It's a real shame that Simon can't figure out the other half of his tatù. With all the boy's potential, there's really no limit as to what he could do...

Gabriel's eyes flickered down the page, to see a hand-drawn recreation of the infamous Kerrigan warlock. An image that had long been burned into his mind, although he had never seen it rendered with such perfect detail.

The clock, for example, was particularly interesting. Had that been there before?

A flicker of anticipation started welling up in his stomach, warming his body like a rogue fire. From the tips of his toes to the tips of his fingers—

—then he slammed the book shut.

Carter's right. Some questions are better left unanswered. It's time to move on.

Without a backwards glance, he tossed the book into the river. It landed with a quiet splash as he turned on his heel and started walking back up the street.

There were people waiting for him now.

It was time to go home.

THE END

Thoughts on Gabriel's Mini-series:

NOTE FROM AUTHOR:
HAPPY ENDINGS ARE JUST stories that haven't finished yet.

I have loved writing this series! It's the first series that I started as an author, and it'll always hold a special place in my heart. The Chronicles of Kerrigan originally started out with the potential to be three books. (don't laugh!) Well, 12 books in the original series, 6 prequel books, 2 sequel books and 3 Gabriel books later, I'm still willing to continue ? I'd love to move on to more characters (like Molly, and Kraigan).

However, there are a lot of books and readers might feel ready to move on. So let me know what you think! Tell me you need more, you're happy or beg me to simply stop. I would love to hear! Oh, and feel free to drop a review on the site you purchased the story on!

Email: wanitamay@aol.com

FB: https://www.facebook.com/pages/Author-WJ-May-FAN-PAGE/141170442608149

Find W.J. May

Website:
http://www.wanitamay.yolasite.com
Facebook:
https://www.facebook.com/pages/Author-WJ-May-FAN-PAGE/141170442608149
Newsletter:
SIGN UP FOR W.J. May's Newsletter to find out about new releases, updates, cover reveals and even freebies!
http://eepurl.com/97aYf

The Chronicles of Kerrigan

BOOK I - *Rae of Hope* is FREE!
  Book Trailer:
  http://www.youtube.com/watch?v=gILAwXxx8MU
  Book II - *Dark Nebula*
  Book Trailer:
  http://www.youtube.com/watch?v=Ca24STi_bFM
  Book III - *House of Cards*
  Book IV - *Royal Tea*
  Book V - *Under Fire*
  Book VI - *End in Sight*
  Book VII – *Hidden Darkness*
  Book VIII – *Twisted Together*
  Book IX – *Mark of Fate*
  Book X – *Strength & Power*
  Book XI – *Last One Standing*
  BOOK XII – *Rae of Light*

PREQUEL –
Christmas Before the Magic
Question the Darkness

Into the Darkness
Fight the Darkness
Alone the Darkness
Lost the Darkness

STARING AT THE FUTURE

SEQUEL –
Matter of Time
Time Piece
Second Chance
Glitch in Time
Out Time
Precious Time

More books by W.J. May

Hidden Secrets Saga:
**Download Seventh Mark part 1 For FREE
Book Trailer:**
http://www.youtube.com/watch?v=Y-_vVYC1gvo

LIKE MOST TEENAGERS, Rouge is trying to figure out who she is and what she wants to be. With little knowledge about her past, she has questions but has never tried to find the answers. Everything changes when she befriends a strangely intoxicating family. Siblings Grace and Michael, appear to have secrets which seem connected to Rouge. Her hunch is confirmed when a horrible incident occurs at an outdoor party. Rouge may be the only one who can find the answer.

An ancient journal, a Sioghra necklace and a special mark force life-altering decisions for a girl who grew up unprepared to fight for her life or others.

All secrets have a cost and Rouge's determination to find the truth can only lead to trouble...or something even more sinister.

RADIUM HALOS - THE SENSELESS SERIES
Book 1 is FREE:

Everyone needs to be a hero at one point in their life.

The small town of Elliot Lake will never be the same again.

Caught in a sudden thunderstorm, Zoe, a high school senior from Elliot Lake, and five of her friends take shelter in an abandoned uranium mine. Over the next few days, Zoe's hearing sharpens drastically, beyond what any normal human being can detect. She tells her friends, only to learn that four others have an increased sense as well. Only Kieran, the new boy from Scotland, isn't affected.

Fashioning themselves into superheroes, the group tries to stop the strange occurrences happening in their little town. Muggings, break-ins, disappearances, and murder begin to hit too close to home. It leads the team to think someone knows about their secret - someone who wants them all dead.

An incredulous group of heroes. A traitor in the midst. Some dreams are written in blood.

Courage Runs Red

The Blood Red Series
Book 1 is FREE

WHAT IF COURAGE WAS your only option?

When Kallie lands a college interview with the city's new hot-shot police officer, she has no idea everything in her life is about to change. The detective is young, handsome and seems to have an unnatural ability to stop the increasing local crime rate. Detective Liam's particular interest in Kallie sends her heart and head stumbling over each other.

When a raging blood feud between vampires spills into her home, Kallie gets caught in the middle. Torn between love and family loyalty she must find the courage to fight what she fears the most and possibly risk everything, even if it means dying for those she loves.

STARING AT THE FUTURE

Daughter of Darkness - Victoria

Only Death Could Stop Her Now

The Daughters of Darkness is a series of female heroines who may or may not know each other, but all have the same father, Vlad Montour.

Victoria is a Hunter Vampire

TUDOR COMPARISON:

AUMBRY HOUSE—A recess to hold sacred vessels, often found in castle chapels.

Aumbry House was considered very special to hold the female students - their sacred vessels (especially Rae Kerrigan).

Joist House—A timber stretched from wall-to-wall to support floorboards.

Joist House was considered a building of support where the male students could support and help each other.

Oratory—A private chapel in a house.

Private education room in the school where the students were able to practice their gifting and improve their skills. Also used as a banquet - dance hall when needed.

Oriel—A projecting window in a wall; originally a form of porch, often of wood. The original bay windows of the Tudor period. Guilder College majority of windows were oriel.

Rae often felt her life was being watching through one of these windows. Hence the constant reference to them.

Refectory—A communal dining hall. Same termed used in Tudor times.

Scriptorium—A Medieval writing room in which scrolls were also housed.

Used for English classes and still store some of the older books from the Tudor reign (regarding tatùs).

Privy Council—Secret council and "arm of the government" similar to the CIA, etc... In Tudor times, the Privy Council was King Henry's board of advisors and helped run the country.

Don't miss out!

Click the button below and you can sign up to receive emails whenever W.J. May publishes a new book. There's no charge and no obligation.

https://books2read.com/r/B-A-SSF-PYXO

BOOKS 2 READ

Connecting independent readers to independent writers.

Did you love *Staring at the Future*? Then you should read *The Chronicles of Kerrigan Prequel Series Books #1-3* by W.J. May!

A Boxset collection of the first 3 books in the Chronicles of Kerrigan Prequel Series! Fall in love with USA TODAY Bestselling author, W.J. May's international bestselling series. Learn how it all began... before the magic of tatùs.

Christmas Before the Magic - Book #1

When Argyle invites his best friend, Simon Kerrigan, home for the Christmas holidays, he wants to save Simon from staying at Guilder Boarding School on his own.

Simon comes along and doesn't expect to find much more excitement in the tiny Scottish town where Argyle's family lives. Until he meets Beth, Argyle's older sister. She's beautiful, brash and clearly interested in him. When her father warns him to stay away from her, Simon tries, but sometimes destiny has a hope of it's own.

Question the Darkness – Book #2

Learn how it all began ... before Rae Kerrigan.

The sins of the father are the sins of the son.

What did Rae's father do that put fear in people's eyes at the name Kerrigan?

Simon Kerrigan is a bright kid. He likes to ask questions and push adults in their way of thinking. He's falling for a girl he's been warned to stay away from. Tempted by forbidden love, he also must face the biggest challenge of his life: receive a tattoo on his sixteenth birthday.

This ink is going to give him a supernatural ability unlike anyone before him. When secrets of the past begin to reveal themselves, he questions everything he's ever known.

Pressure from Guilder Boarding School and the Privy Council only confuse Simon more as he struggles to find himself.

How hard will he have to shake the family tree to find the truth about the past?

The Chronicles of Kerrigan Prequel is the beginning of the story before Rae Kerrigan. Christmas Before the Magic is just the beginning (but not the end...)

Into the Darkness – Book #3

What did Rae's father do that put fear in people's eyes at the name Kerrigan?

After a mysterious attempt is made on his life, Simon Kerrigan has more questions than ever, and this time, he's not the only one. The beginnings of a secret society are formed at Guilder. A society of other like-minded students all unsatisfied with the status quo. All searching for the truth.

But things aren't always as they seem.
When Simon gets an unexpected visitor, his entire world is turned upside-down. Suddenly, the rules that were made to keep him safe, are the only things standing in his way.

Who can he trust? Can he learn to master his tatù? Most importantly, can he do it in time to protect those things that are most precious to him?

Also by W.J. May

Bit-Lit Series
Lost Vampire
Cost of Blood
Price of Death

Blood Red Series
Courage Runs Red
The Night Watch
Marked by Courage
Forever Night

Daughters of Darkness: Victoria's Journey
Victoria
Huntress
Coveted (A Vampire & Paranormal Romance)
Twisted

Hidden Secrets Saga
Seventh Mark - Part 1
Seventh Mark - Part 2
Marked By Destiny

Compelled
Fate's Intervention
Chosen Three
The Hidden Secrets Saga: The Complete Series

Paranormal Huntress Series
Never Look Back
Coven Master
Alpha's Permission

Prophecy Series
Only the Beginning
White Winter
Secrets of Destiny

The Chronicles of Kerrigan
Rae of Hope
Dark Nebula
House of Cards
Royal Tea
Under Fire
End in Sight
Hidden Darkness
Twisted Together
Mark of Fate
Strength & Power
Last One Standing
Rae of Light
The Chronicles of Kerrigan Box Set Books # 1 - 6

The Chronicles of Kerrigan: Gabriel
Living in the Past
Staring at the Future
Present For Today

The Chronicles of Kerrigan Prequel
Christmas Before the Magic
Question the Darkness
Into the Darkness
Fight the Darkness
Alone in the Darkness
Lost in Darkness
The Chronicles of Kerrigan Prequel Series Books #1-3

The Chronicles of Kerrigan Sequel
A Matter of Time
Time Piece
Second Chance
Glitch in Time
Our Time
Precious Time

The Hidden Secrets Saga
Seventh Mark (part 1 & 2)

The Senseless Series
Radium Halos

Radium Halos - Part 2
Nonsense

Standalone
Shadow of Doubt (Part 1 & 2)
Five Shades of Fantasy
Shadow of Doubt - Part 1
Shadow of Doubt - Part 2
Four and a Half Shades of Fantasy
Dream Fighter
What Creeps in the Night
Forest of the Forbidden
HuNted
Arcane Forest: A Fantasy Anthology
Ancient Blood of the Vampire and Werewolf

Made in the USA
Lexington, KY
03 October 2018